"Very Informative"

The contents are definitely worth it and I am very impressed.

Germaine Anderson, The Homeschool Bookmark

I love reading your book. Very informative and it is one of the best among many I purchased about homeschooling.

Zsolt, NH

How is it possible that Lorraine Curry wrote in one book what others have attempted in so many?

Deborah Deggs Cariker, former Houston area star reporter

I thoroughly enjoyed reading your **EasyHomeschooling Techniques (Christian edition),** *even with all the religious references. Had it been available and had I realized I could teach my own children at home I certainly would have used it as a guide.*

Rebecca Brown, www.rebeccasreads.com

I've been devouring **Easy Homeschooling Companion.** *Thank you for writing it! I'm also re-reading* **Easy Homeschooling Techniques** *today. Both titles are giving (re-giving) me the direction that I'm needing! THANK YOU!!*

Deb, NE

My doubts disappeared, replaced with a peace, knowing that I made the right choice. I thank you so much for the "tools."

Jo Ann

I LOVE my book. . . . Thank you for getting me thinking, re-organized and motivated again!!
    Pat, GA

The book was wonderful. . . . Thank you for the encourage-ment and push into the right direction.
    Debbie Burkett

Easy Homeschooling Techniques *by Lorraine Curry has some unique aspects I have seen in no other homeschooling* **book.**
    Mary Collis, Home School Favourites, Australia

I have read chapter 1 about 20 times! It is the one book that I am recommending to anyone considering homeschooling. The book is one of those life-changing books—if you read it and follow its guidelines, it will change your life (unless you already do all of this). If I had one word to describe what the book teaches it would be "focus."
    Edie Molder

I absolutely LOVE this book! I already have a copy, but I often lend it out, and then I really miss it!
    Linda, CA

I have read it twice! After seven years of homeschooling I have learned that the most expensive or most time consum-ing teaching method is not always the best. Your book makes that SO clear. It was also very encouraging.
    Millie, CA

I just got the sample copy, and sat down and read two sections . . . the ones on methods and home businesses. If the rest of the book is this good, you've got a winner.
    Mary Hood, *The Relaxed Home Schooler*

Bite-size, manageable chapters bursting with information . . . something for everyone.
> Shari Henry, author of *Homeschooling: The Middle Years*

It was your book that made it look so easy to homeschool, that my daughter and I are pulling my three grandchildren out of public school.
> Patricia A. Saye, "Lady Liberty"

Wealth of important information.
> Kathy Reynolds, *The Home School Gazette*

I LOVE your book!!!!
> Penni, MA

It is wonderful! It gives real, simple advice that can help avoid burnout while homeschooling.
> Debbie, IL

I've gotten so much encouragement from your book. . . . God bless you.
> Renee

An EXCELLENT resource for beginning homeschoolers and veterans alike! Highly recommended.
> Robin Nash, The Mustard Seed

A superb job.
> Laurie Hicks, author of *Simply Phonics* & *Simply Spelling*

Lorraine Curry has a gift for making homeschooling easy! This book is no exception. Chapters are short, manageable for the mom needing help and needing it QUICKLY! Whether you are new to homeschooling, wanting to get off to a good start; or you have homeschooled for more years than you can count, this book will have much to offer. I found myself making excuses to curl up to read just ONE more chapter!

www.lifetimebooksandgifts.com

I can't remember if I let you know how much I LOVE your book! It was such a breath of fresh air! I have been VERY impressed with it. It was such a delight for me. You KNOW it is a great book when a veteran is just as encouraged as a newbie!

Cindy Rushton, author, publisher of *Time for Tea*

I guess my excitement stems from the many books I've read and gotten nowhere with . . . something about the way yours is written . . . your book spoke to me in a way that none of the others have . . . it's so easy to follow—all the symbols you put in there to mark what goes in a notebook were very helpful.

Dee, FL

Lots of great stuff. Many more goodies than just techniques for teaching. Lorraine believes that home education does not have to mimic institutional school . . . also doesn't believe in letting students "do their own thing" without accountability. Methods are quite similar to Charlotte Mason with an emphasis on lots of reading and research. Tells HOW to implement a low stress education without blowing the budget. I learned new things, and it reaffirmed several points on which I was shaky . . . definitely worth a read, and a re-read at that.

Virginia Knowles, *The Hope Chest*

Easy Homeschooling

Boelus NE 68820 USA

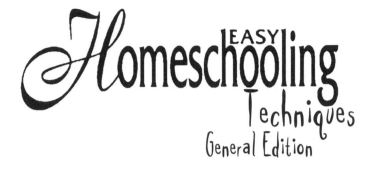

EASY
Homeschooling
Techniques
General Edition

by Lorraine Curry

with Naomi Aldort Ph. D., Janice Campbell & Cathi-Lyn Dyck

Easy Homeschooling Techniques
General Edition

Definitions, unless otherwise specified, are derived from the *American Heritage Electronic Dictionary* © 1993, Houghton, Mifflin Co.

Book design, layout and illustration—Lorraine Curry

Chapter 8 illustrations—Lorraine Curry from *Fields with God.*

Chapter 14 illustrations—Cathi-Lyn Dyck

"Jessica's Favorites" booklist—Jessica Curry Jobes

"SpillMilk"— Ethan/www.fonthead.com

Dedicated To You!

You are a special group of people—you give so much daily for your children. Because of your decision to homeschool, someday your mature, young adults will set their sails, having had the very best foundation, ready to be assets to the world. Congratulations for what you have done, are doing and will do!

With Special Thanks To

My Very Able Contributors & Editors

Naomi Aldort
Janice Campbell
Cathi-Lyn Dyck
Jean Hall
Marilyn Rockett

Contents

10. Teaching Writing . . . 125

By Janice Campbell

Readiness • Reading • Copying • Narration • Dictation • Composition • The Ben Franklin Method • Creative Writing • Evaluating Writing

Authors and Poets . . . 129

11. Mining Methods and History . . . 145

Greeks • Romans • Classical Homeschooling • Renaissance • Primary School • Milton • Rousseau • Pestalozzi • Charlotte Mason Homeschooling • Wilderspin • Herbart • Froebel • Mann • Dewey • Unschooling • Relaxed • The Moore Method • The Robinson Method

12. Building a Business . . . 165

Family Business • Be Ready • Choose Right • Achieve Success • Market • Network • Advertise • Homeschool while Working • Tips from Working Moms

13. Sailing through High School . . . 179

Greater Literature • Yes, Read Aloud • Independent Study • Science and Math • Keep Credit Hours • College • Life Skills • World of Options

14. Getting Truly Critical . . . 189

By Cathi-Lyn Dyck

Assumptions • Basis • Values and Beliefs • Desires • Starting Young

Are you Qualified?

❏ I love my children.
❏ I have, or can make, some time each day to spend with them.
❏ I have strong beliefs not taught in public schools.
❏ I can probably do better than public schools.
❏ I can read and write.
❏ I usually commit to things I believe in.

Did you check most of the boxes? You are qualified to homeschool!

Dingbat Key

✔ Teaching tip or technique
✘ General tip or technique
•◦ Notebook activity
☆ Especially important statement
❀ See more in *Easy Homeschooling Companion*
✍ Vintage or out of print book
☞ If bolded, look in the back of the book

What Children Should Be Taught

- To cook plain wholesome food
- To care for his or her own room
- That it is better to be useful than ornamental
- That the old rule, "A place for everything and everything in its place," is a good one
- That he or she should dress for health and comfort as well as for appearance
- To respect gray hairs
- To be gentle
- To be courteous
- To be prompt
- To be industrious
- To be truthful
- To be thoughtful and attentive
- To do all kinds of housework
- To earn money and to take care of it
- To be neat and orderly in his or her habits and appearance
- To be self-reliant

Adapted from *Home and Health* © 1907, Pacific Press

Foreword

When Lorraine sent me an earlier edition of this book, I sat down and read the whole thing, which I didn't really have time to do. I had the feeling I was reading all the how-to books boiled down into one volume.

This book is concise; Lorraine won't waste your time telling you things you already know. But she will show you how to keep school from being an expensive, confusing operation that leaves you tearing your hair out. She has included detailed courses of study for each grade, excerpts from vintage books, author and poet lists, schedule planners and a list of free or inexpensive resources. Briefly and clearly, she explains how to make sense of various homeschooling methods, lay a good foundation and set goals that you can meet. She'll give you ways to tell if you are qualified to homeschool, identify time robbers, help you choose good literature for your children and encourage you to read classic novels to even your youngest children. She'll help you see you can learn to draw and paint with your children and why it's important. She even discusses cleaning, teaching with old books and old-fashioned methods!

I loved this book! Reading it may give you the confidence you've been needing. A wonderful gift for a new or veteran homeschooler. It would be a special comfort to someone who is being pressured by family or friends and has begun to lose sight of the big picture.

Tammy Duby
www.tobinslab.com

Preface

I forced open my heavy eyelids and looked around the dimly lit room. Would that baby ever stop crying? The pale green walls were about to enfold me in deep sleep. But wait—that was my baby! It had to be! The tiny hospital's nursery had been empty as we passed earlier that evening.

Soon that baby was snuggled quietly in my arms, and I was in the midst of life's most wondrous experience. Before long, three other precious children were placed under our sheltering wings. How then could we tear them out from that protected place and entrust their care and education to anyone else? No one else could love them as we did!

But me?—a *teacher*? I never wanted anything to do with education! My fondness for art and design made "education" seem bland and boring.

★ **However, my children's well being was more important than my inclinations.** Yet, I still refused to consider a structured curriculum. Simple techniques evolved that resulted in children rich in skills and knowledge.

A Practical Guide for the Beginner

This book was written as a technique manual for the beginner. It begins at the beginning, details simple techniques and gives step-by-step instructions. It answers questions such as these:

- "What do I buy?"
- "What can I skip?"
- "How can I simplify the methods, materials and advice?"
- "What do I do first?"
- "How do I do it?"
- "Why should I avoid a structured or full curriculum?"
- "Can I really homeschool through high school?"

You will soon learn how to start and operate a homeschool that will rival the best schools in the nation. This book explains the "nuts and bolts" of the method called Easy Homeschooling. You can homeschool whether you are rich, poor, poorly educated or even employed outside of your home—and the payoff is excellence, with minimal effort. ☆ **Do not spend a dime, or saddle yourself with unnecessary stress, until you read this book!**

A Better Way for the Experienced

Are you already homeschooling? Do you feel overwhelmed because of what you think you must do to educate your children? Are you marooned on Methods Island, trying to make sense of them all? Are you drowning under a deluge of educational materials? The catalogs keep getting bigger and bigger while the decisions become more and more difficult. Even reading the giant curriculum guides takes valuable time.

Are you using a structured curriculum? Do you really enjoy your lessons—and their preparation? Are the courses pushing too much? Are your children really learning anything?

Perhaps you have been using the unit study approach. How much time do you spend in preparation? And in "school"? Is this much time really necessary for quality education?

Are you searching for a method that will draw your family closer? Independent studies and computer courses can pull family members in different directions.

Which method will draw your family closer?

Materials

Have you ever gone to a store needing one item and found yourself detained hesitating among an overwhelming array of manufacturers' brands? The vast assortment of homeschooling materials now available can make things extremely confusing. Homeschooling doesn't have to be so complicated! Easy Homeschooling is a simple—yet high quality—method of educating. Moreover, this method offers tips and suggestions for low-cost alternatives. Homeschooling can even be free! This book tells how. But because most of us want to purchase some books and materials, I give certain materials a stamp of approval. But the choice—whether to spend or not to spend—is yours!

Do you want to be frugal or free with cash?

Three Basic Methods

The maze of methods can be simplified by sorting them into three basic groups: unschooling, structured schooling and a style of schooling that I will call watershed schooling.

Unschooling

John Holt—whose books are available at libraries—was the father of unschooling, the first method of the modern homeschooling movement. Bill Greer of ☞ *F.U.N. News* says that unschoolers want "to keep alive the spark of curiosity and the natural love of learning with which all children are born."[1]

The idea behind unschooling is that individuals learn best when they are free to seek knowledge about personal interests. I found this true in my own life. My knowledge store accumulated only when I had a personal interest in—and sought out information about—a particular subject. The sum of what I learned during structured schooling could have been taught in a year or two. (If there had been more reading aloud from interesting books throughout my youth, things might have been different!)

Unschooling is a hands-off method. In pure unschooling the parent acts as teacher only when the child expresses interest in a particular topic—then merely aids the child in finding the resources he or she needs. Mark and Helen Hegener, publisher and editor of ☞ *Home Education Magazine,* say:

> *Our children have always been completely responsible for their own learning, from the ABC's on up. They've known from day one that they've had our complete and loving support, and that we'd be here to help them whenever they asked for it. There's been no delineation in our family between "learning" and "living." As we live, we learn. It's as simple as that.*[2]

Dr. Raymond and Dorothy Moore in their book, ☞ *The Successful Homeschool Family Handbook*, report on a well-funded study done many years ago which gives a gold star to unschooling. "The children who were not formally taught at all had the highest scores in all areas measured."[3]

Structured Schooling

Most of us know structured schooling well because we are its products! Structured homeschoolers have just moved the school into their homes—sometimes even moved a teacher into their homes through the use of videos. The structured homeschoolers purchase their books, materials and teacher's guides from one company or from similar curriculum companies. Such books usually have an abundance of data in them that the students are expected to read and retain, but alas! Students promptly forget most everything they have read. I know—I was schooled this way and also witnessed our daughters' lack of retention when they used these books. Although the books are sometimes beautiful and interesting, permanent learning is rare with a structured curriculum.

Watershed Schooling

A watershed is a ridge of high land dividing two areas that are drained by different river systems. A watershed is also a critical point that marks a division. I'm dubbing this group "watershed" because it is midway between unschooling and structured schooling. Watershed parents usually, in their own words, pick and choose curricula. Some make their own plans and schedules and teach whatever they want. Others loosely follow the plan of a chosen method. They sometimes focus on the child's interest—as in unschooling—but more often the teacher decides what she wants her children to learn. She may have a schedule or may just do school when it is convenient. These parents are usually flexible in what, where, why and how, and yet not so flexible that they give the child complete control—as in pure unschooling. Often much time is spent in reading aloud. There are more homeschoolers in this third group than in any other.[4] Some examples are *Charlotte Mason* and *Easy Homeschooling*.

Easy Homeschooling

Although other methods have given good results, all methods are not equal. Easy Homeschooling techniques such as planning, combining, using the library and reading aloud unite to produce high quality education without large expenditures of time or money.

Just as Easy Homeschooling provides maximum education in minimum time, the mission of this book is to provide maximum information in a minimum of words. I have chosen to leave out socialization and laws, as well as lengthy personal experiences, so that I can focus on what *you* will do in your own successful homeschool. By following the suggestions in this book, you will save its price many, many times over. May *Easy Homeschooling Techniques* inspire your thoughts and actions and be always completely usable.

Lorraine Curry
www.easyhomeschooling.com

Note: *Since you will be learning with your children, I have used the pronoun, "you" interchangeably to represent you or your children. Many times you will want to have your child do the suggested activity. Other times you will do it together.*

1
Laying Foundations

I lay on the beach, gasping for breath. I was a body surfer and even Maui's huge winter storm waves couldn't keep me home! The exhilaration was worth the battering. In college, I wanted to skydive, but my father wouldn't grant permission—a friend's son had been killed when his parachute failed to open. Later, I was enticed by the opportunity to succeed in life insurance sales and became the first female member of our company's President's Cabinet. I've welcomed most challenges, but succeeding at this task of raising children has been life's biggest challenge—and its greatest adventure.

By definition, an adventure is an undertaking that includes uncertainty. Are you asking yourself, "Is homeschooling the best choice for my child? . . . Can I *really* do this?" I never really considered whether I was qualified to teach my own children. My desire to keep them home was so strong, I knew that I would find a way.

An adventure is often—by its uncertain nature—an exciting experience. There are surprises ahead that you don't even know about yet!

Homeschooling can be a financial speculation or risk—somewhat like a business venture. The word "speculation" makes it sound as if homeschooling is risky. But homeschoolers everywhere prove that this venture is a good thing!

There are several good reasons to homeschool. I wanted my children to have a better education than I had. I felt like we could do better than the schools. Why do you want to homeschool?

Notebook Planning

➼ Get a notebook or diary. You can use a three-ring binder, loose-leaf notebook paper and at least five tabbed dividers or a thick divided spiral notebook. I have a *Busy Woman's Daily Planner* with pages that seem to be made for this system. For help in choosing the planner and pages that will work best for you call 800-848-7715 or visit *www.thebusywoman.com*.

Write your motives (reasons) for wanting to homeschool on the first page of your notebook. I think you will enjoy this list-making process! These planning techniques will build a foundation that will make homeschooling easier and more focused.[1]

Now go to the second page and make a list of your values. A value is *a principle, standard, or quality considered worthwhile or desirable.* Some values are a strong family, a consistently loving attitude and untarnished integrity.

Dream Dreams

➼ Label your first index tab "Dreams." List your dreams for yourself and your family. This activity should be done over a period of time, such as several days. Keep adding to your list. Make sure you have everything, even those dreams that seem totally out of reach. Think big!
My lists include the following:

- I would see my children grown into fine young adults.
- I would be a designer in my own manufacturing company.
- I would write and publish several books, including an autobiography, how-to's and novels.

This list gives ideas and examples of the types of dreams that you can put on your list. Look over your own dreams list and check to see if your dreams are in line with your values. Either cross off those that aren't or star those that are. But don't be too hasty—another name for dreams is desires.

Set Goals

Goals are definite results that can be achieved within a certain period of time. Long-term goals might be achieved within five years; short-term within one. No need to list your long-term and short-term goals separately. These lists work. After three months, I had achieved almost half of my top goals; after six, I crossed off more!

- ~~Start up business.~~
- ~~Run business.~~
- ~~Become organized.~~
- ~~Sell land.~~
- ~~Pay off credit cards.~~
- Teach children to be self starters.
- Finish restoring house.

This is not my complete goal list. I have combined major goals for illustration purposes. Several completed goals will lead to fulfillment of your dreams. Again, take time to get your thoughts crystallized. Don't rush this process. When you get your goals down on paper and see a pattern emerging, it will be clearer why you have considered homeschooling.

Your goals for your children could be that they have inner peace, a passion for ending war or other social issues, that they become a contributing citizen, that they have high character, self-discipline or find their life purpose.

➾ Label your second index divider "Goals." Following the examples, list your own goals. You may make separate lists of personal goals, homeschooling goals and business goals, along with any goals you may have set for each of your children. Choose your top ten goals from your lists and star each or list these top goals on a separate piece of paper. These will be the goals that you will work on first. Place this list in the front of your goal section. If you have made lists for your children, choose one or two important goals for each of them.

At least once a year, review and revise both your dream list and your goal list. At that time you may decide that a particular dream or goal wasn't as important as you once thought. Eliminate it from your list and replace it with any new dreams and goals you want to add.

Commitment

Next, it is time to consider commitment. If we go into a major personal relationship without commitment, the relationship usually fails. Homeschooling also requires serious commitment. Decide what you want for your family. This is *such* an important step! If you will not commit, I cannot wholeheartedly recommend homeschooling. Your child might be better off elsewhere.

There is a method for reaching your goals. There are steps to take that will lead to the fulfillment of your dreams. In Chapter 5, "Planning for Success," you will learn how to schedule those steps. When you work your step lists, your goals will be met and surpassed, almost automatically. Decide to commit to homeschooling. This book will make your commitment effortless, as you discover that homeschooling can be simple and natural.

➼ Enter your commitment statement or pledge on the very first page of your notebook along with your motive statement.

Educational Philosophy

Why educate? If you have read about home education, you may have already formulated some opinions, but don't be too quick to define your educational philosophy. An example is Charlotte Mason's. She said, "It is the business of education to find some way of supplementing the weakness of will which is the bane of most of us, as of the children."[2]

Here's another:

> *An education isn't how much you have committed to memory, or even how much you know. It's being able to differentiate between what you do know and what you don't. It's knowing where to go to find out what you need to know; and it's knowing how to use the information once you get it. . . .*[3]

For more ideas on the philosophy of education, see Chapter 11, "Mining Methods & History."

➤ After you have formulated your educational philosophy, write it in the front pages of your notebook. When you have laid the foundation by listing your motives, commitment pledge, educational philosophy and values in the first pages of your notebook and your dreams and goals in their own sections, you are ready to go on and start your very own successful homeschool. However, if you have not done all of the above, you can still jump in and be successful!

Why should we then educate?

2
Starting Up

*Z*ephi, at five, amazed her aunt and uncle with her perfect reading. "Perhaps," my public-school-educator sister offered, "she should have the advantages of the special resources of schools." Although I highly respected her opinions and had been greatly influenced by her previously, this time the call to homeschooling was stronger than her advice. The fact is, the mother is the perfect teacher for her own children because she loves them more than anyone else ever could. The father, of course, is also qualified and responsible for teaching his own children.

Can you read? You can teach your children to read. Can you write? You can teach them to write. You can teach your children to teach themselves, even though you may not know a subject well. You can read and learn, and share what you've learned. You can learn along with them! Qualifications to guide your children into educational excellence are minimal.

Legal Requirements

Homeschooling is legal in every state and province in Canada. Information can be obtained from your state's or province's Department of Education or from the ☞ **Home School Legal Defense Association.** Some homeschooling books include this information—but be sure it is current. I found outdated legal requirements in our library's copy of ☞ *The Home School Manual* by Theodore Wade.

Some states might allow you to choose what day of the year, days of the week and hours of the day you want to homeschool. Along with a minimum number of hours required, you might also need to sign and notarize forms. Some states require a scope and sequence if one does not use a recognized curriculum. A scope and sequence details what one plans to teach each year and in what order the topics will be presented. See Chapter 5, "Planning for Success," for more about the scope and sequence, including instructions for creating it.

If the parent uses a structured curriculum package from a major publisher, a scope and sequence may not be required. Although this may be easier when submitting information, the day-to-day use of a full curriculum is definitely more difficult and time-consuming. It is also the same ineffective style of educating that has been used in schools for years. This method attempts to pour facts and figures into the student, hoping that some will "stick." It allows no room for individuality, but rather molds each student into a "clone" of the next one. Since I am a creative type, I hated this type of education as a youth and wasn't about to tackle it, nor shackle my children with it. With *Easy Homeschooling,* you can forget the bother and expense of using a traditional curriculum with its hefty and formidable teacher's guides!

Prepare!

Before you actually start schooling, some preparations need to be made. Along with making time, there is "preschool"—but this preschool is not what you would expect! There is also the preparation of organizing the home which you will learn in Chapter 4, "Making Order." Because this startup is so easy and gradual, you can delay your organization until later, but if you feel you just must have order now, jump to Chapter 4 first, and then come back here.

Make Time

If homeschooling is started with young children, there is a gradual building of routines—and very little time required—because subjects can be introduced one at a time.[1]

If you are taking your child out of an institutional school, there might be more time required, but not as much as you might think. To make more time, set your priorities and eliminate distractions.

Disconnect the Distractions

TV and videos are time robbers. Although there are a few worthwhile programs and videos, the value of these—in my opinion—can never outweigh their detriment. Thirty years of research show that ninety percent of achievement in school is determined by how much TV a child watches.[2] The separate hemispheres of the brain have different functions. If one is stimulated more in the developmental stage (from ages two to twelve), the other could be stunted. The nature of TV dumbs down children, causing short attention span and creating the need for simplistic (instead of rich and classic) subject matter. Other negative effects on children are less sensitivity to the pain and suffering of others, greater fear of the world around them and increased likelihood of engaging in aggressive or harmful behavior. Many of you know exactly what I am talking about, because you have seen these effects in your own children. Consider these facts and predictions from *The Futurist* magazine:

> *Television is absorbing increasing amounts of people's free time . . . . [It is] entertainment without any need to associate with other people. . . . [It] deprives people of the social learning acquired during group entertainment. In the days before television and computers, face-to-face conversation was the primary means of entertainment, pursued around the dinner table at home. . . . This social entertainment trained people to deal with other people, to respect their interests . . . . The rise of electronic entertainment seems to have been ac-*

companied by increasing rudeness . . . will tend to desocialize
people, making them more prone to antisocial and criminal
behavior . . . a non-society—a poorly integrated mass of elec-
tronic hermits, unable to work well together because we no
longer play together. Institutions . . . will face the challenge
of seeking support from people whose loyalty is almost en-
tirely to themselves.[3]

Along with TV, computers and online activities can also interfere with
family solidarity, and waste time. Soon after World War II, science
fiction writings predicted "that people might become the slaves of
machines . . . might begin to think differently, submit to computers,
lose judgment, become spiritually shallow, unhappy and unable to cope
with jobs and daily lives dominated by technology."[4]

Having a computer requires self-control and wisdom. Contrary to
popular opinion, it is not essential for a quality education. Your child
will learn computer skills quickly when needed. There are so many
better things to do—books to read, walks and picnics to go on, chores
to do together, independent discovery—the list is endless.

Other Time Robbers

Do you (or your children) spend a lot of time reading catalogs or magazines? Are your days spent on the telephone or shopping? Life is too
short to waste.

Plan to spend the greatest portion of your time
on the activites that will help you reach your goals.
In Chapter 5, you will learn to list these activities as steps to your goals (step lists).

➤ Take a one- or two-week inventory of
exactly how you spend every hour of every
day. You may see a whole lot of time that
could be better spent.

If you have many small children and
many demands on your life, hang on—
it does get easier! Our four children were

very close in age, so I know what some of you are going through. But our girls started helping at a young age, and eventually did so much of the housework that I was able to do projects such as book writing! There is a time and season for everything. Which brings me to counsel you not to rush into homeschooling when your children are too young. How do you know when they are too young? Resistance to instruction is a good sign. Be sensitive to your child. Most of all, *enjoy* those precious little ones—how I long to be able to return to those days you are now experiencing. They are truly the best days of your life!

Easy Preschool

You have prepared by thinking, listening, listing, making time and possibly making order. Now we will begin schooling. You don't have to leave home. You don't have to buy toys, games or snacks. You don't have to expose your children to other children's germs. At this preschool you cuddle in with your little ones and read lots of good books. That's it! This is the *Easy Homeschooling* preschool. Simple, isn't it?

You do not have to spend hundreds of dollars when you begin to homeschool. Do not overwhelm yourself and your child with an excess of material. Easy does it. The best materials are often those that you already have in your home. You really don't need a lot.

Read To Your Children

Professionals and intellectuals agree that the most important thing parents can do for their child's education is to read to them. The one common factor found in all children who learned to read without being formally taught was not high IQ, not high family income, not parents who had college degrees, but rather "all these children were read to by their parents regularly, frequently, and from whatever materials happened to be at hand—newspapers, road signs, even packing labels."[5]

If you do an abundance of reading aloud, your children will learn spelling, grammar, vocabulary and style without being formally taught.

It may be—especially if your child has watched much TV or many videos—that he or she will find it difficult to concentrate when you read aloud. If this is the case, ban video and start reading simple books on an interesting subject. The longer the fast from visual stimulation, the more their hunger for words develops. They will desire the mental stimulation of words and the enjoyable process of making their own mind pictures. May I suggest Beatrix Potter's well written and illustrated titles such as *Peter Rabbit*. Other options are vintage books about animals by Thornton Burgess (reprints available from ☞ **Dover**) or Arthur Scott Bailey (*www.hstreasures.com*). These will hold a young child's interest, expand intelligence and whet his appetite for good books.

An easy startup technique is to introduce the basics one at a time. Make sure your child knows phonics well before going on to reading. When he can read fluently, begin handwriting exercises. Creative writing can only be done after handwriting is learned. (Pre-writing *can* be done and is explained below.) Finally, begin simple math. An exception is combining spelling with phonics. See more in Chapter 6, "Combining Subjects."

Early childhood is the best time to begin establishing and maintaining habits—especially health habits such as brushing and flossing teeth, bathing regularly and washing face and hands as needed.

Phonics

Achievement in all subjects will be built upon thoughtful reading. Skill in reading starts with a mastery of phonics. Public education's failure is most obvious in this area as parents often purchase phonics materials and reteach their children the most basic of skills—when the school has had all day to do it. Look at what else parents are supposed to do.

[They should] . . . talk to their children about school and homework, read with them, go to the library, have books at home and ensure

that their children attend school daily. "I'd like parents to go into the school and be involved with the teacher, the principal, the PTA . . . ."[6]

Whew! Talk about overtaxing already stressed parents! You will do it right the first time by teaching your child yourself. Although the "No Child Left Behind" program has attempted to solve the problems, according to recent reports it is experiencing "growing pains."

The Reading Solution

The solution to the reading problem is phonics. We used the same copy of ☞ **Alpha-phonics** by Samuel Blumenfeld for each of our children. Actually I used it for only three of our four, because Zephi sat in on her older sister's lessons and learned to read on her own. Several years ago, the book cost us around twenty dollars. It was one of our best buys considering the great value of reading and the per-student cost. The book was very easy to use. ☞ **Simply Phonics** is similar to *Alpha-Phonics*. It can be used for one to three years and will take your child step by step through letter sounds and word families. When your child finishes the book, he or she is able to read!

Soon your child will be able to read!

✔ A free *Easy Homeschooling* technique is to do it yourself without a book. Start with the lower case (small) letters because text is primarily lower case. Later your child will learn to read the upper case.

Using a pencil and paper (or a dry-erase marker board or chalk board), teach the sound of each letter, starting with the short vowels. Always speak to your young children as clearly as possible! Add some consonants—one at a time—to make simple words such as *cat* and *dog*. Next teach the vowel combinations such as *ea* and *oi*. Other consonant combinations such as *ch* and *st* should be taught along with

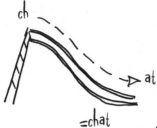

all the rest of the consonants. Finally, teach long vowels, long vowel combinations and words with silent e at the end such as "gate."

To help your child blend the sounds of letters into words, use a simple playground slide diagram. At the top of the slide write the beginning letter or combination, and at the bottom, the rest of the word. "Make the 'ch' go down the slide and run into the 'at'!" Keep it simple by teaching only the sounds of the letters. Later your child can learn the names—perhaps when long vowels are learned. Teach the usual sounds of the letters—do not confuse your child by teaching rules or exceptions now. If they ask, just tell them they will learn those later, identifying them as "rule breakers." If your little geniuses are really interested in these exceptions, have them list them in a notebook!

Following is a simplified sequence chart for teaching phonics. Teach the sounds consecutively. Make sure your child gets plenty of practice reading words that fit each pattern.

Phonics Chart

- short a, e, i, o, u; and y sounding as a short vowel

- consonant sounds (all the rest of the letters)

- consonant clusters such as ch, th, st

- broad o: au, aw, al

- other clusters: oi, oy, ou, ow; oo; ar, er, ir, or, ur

- long vowel clusters: ea, ee, ai, oa, ow

- long vowels: words that end in silent e

- c followed by e, i or y says "s"

- g followed by e, i or y may say "j"

✓ For drill, make your own flash cards. Use three-by-five inch blank index cards, scrap cardboard or white poster board cut to size. Write one large letter or combination (*sh, pl, ch,* etc.) on each card. Have your child say the sound. Later put these cards together to form simple words.

Practice Makes Perfect

As soon as your child knows how to read, he or she needs practice. Get simple phonics-based readers such as *Hop on Pop* from the library or *Bob Books* from ☞ **Scholastic.** But don't try to use *Dick and Jane*! These books have so many sight words in them, they will only frustrate your new reader. By using *McGuffey's Readers*—received free as an introductory offer from a book club—our girls were two grade levels ahead of other homeschoolers when they were in second grade. They were then reading independently and fluently, so we discontinued *McGuffeys* but kept them for their content. The secret to success with whatever practice materials you choose is regularity. Do something every day, even if it's just for a short time.

Some educational "authorities" would burden us with unnecessary work such as spelling, comprehension, grammar and vocabulary. These do not need to be learned separately! If a child is read to, learns to read phonetically, *is read to,* starts reading fluently, *is read to,* and continues to read individually, that child will learn, and learn well, all the peripherals of our language.

Penmanship

Don't be confused by the styles available. Just choose one and stick with it. We started with traditional and then went to italic. Since our eldest had started with regular cursive she did not do well with italic so we went back to regular cursive for her. All of our other children used italic  workbooks. Zephi did calligraphy at eleven. At age fifteen, Jessica finally acquired an attractive hand after more practice with calligraphy and Spencerian. One complaint I hear from my children who have learned italic is that they can't read cursive, although they do eventually figure it out. Handwriting is important training in neatness and influences achievement in every subject.

✔ Although there are penmanship tablets available, any type of notebook or notebook paper will do. Use two lines or as many as necessary, adapting the size to that which your child is comfortable with. (Have him or her make a letter first so you can see.) In your best penmanship, write the alphabet in a column to the left of the page and let your child fill out the rest of each line. Worksheets for penmanship (and for nearly every other subject) can be printed from internet sites. Search for "free worksheets" along with your topic word at *www.google.com.*

Pre-Writing, Writing

✓ Encourage your youngest children to be storytellers. If your child is not able to write yet, take dictation as he or she tells you the story. Your child can then illustrate their story. This is the creative pre-writing I mentioned earlier. When you read to your children from a young age, they will be natural writers.

Copywork is an effective technique for the young child. Either write the passage for your child to copy or let him copy directly from a book. By doing copywork, your child will learn style and grammar from master writers.

When your children are able to write, have them transcribe their own stories. Don't pay any attention to errors at this point. You don't want to discourage them. If they want you to spell the words for them, do it. Eventually they will know more words. At that time, you can point out misspelled words or make a daily or weekly spelling list of those. (See more on spelling in Chapter 6, "Combining Subjects.") Save your students' papers—at least the best ones. You will treasure them someday! If you need help with grammar, get a language handbook from *www.amazon.com.* You could even use an old or vintage title.

Arithmetic

Children will learn number concepts by taking part in ordinary daily activities. For instance, they can be a big help by counting silverware and setting the table. Some people use beans or other items to teach primary number concepts. Although we used many games and other math materials over the years, we found the simplest tools to be best.

✓ The simplest tools are pencils and paper. Flash cards can be made starting with the easiest equation: 1+1=2. Use daily until the facts are mastered and then occasionally for review. *Calculadder* is a set of master sheets for timed math drills and is effective for mastering the math facts. Another great tool is an antique math text. Save time, money and effort by using speed drills and old texts exclusively for the best results with young students. We had great results with *Strayer-Upton Practical Arithmetics,* which are now available as reprints.

Learn With Your Children

After a degree of mastery has been achieved in the basics, you can continue with every other subject and topic by studying together. Subjects that you might have disliked all of your life suddenly come alive. This was my experience with history. When the children and I started reading biographies and other historical books, I discovered history to be quite interesting!

Your Children Learn With You

As a homeschooler, you will do the sometimes inconvenient thing, and let your child be your partner in every task you and your husband do. This is the most effective training and learning opportunity. If you do it now, you will later see hard-working children, more free time and a closer family. What work can your children do with you? Everything you do!

Learn Together

- Cook
- Clean
- Wash dishes
- Wash clothes
- Decorate
- Sew
- Garden
- Landscape
- Sketch
- Can foods
- Change oil in vehicle

The sky's the limit! You will think of many more ideas, and when you do, do the activity with your children. This is the beauty of homeschooling.

3
Easy School Basics

I dropped the magazine into my lap and gazed into the distance where Jessica, Ezra and Eli were jumping from the bridge piling into the glistening river. I was dazed—and it wasn't the summer sun. Under *structured* on the cover of this "methods" issue was the word, *easiest*. How could it be? How could they say this method was easier than even the highly successful unschooling? A long-time acquaintance—and brand new homeschooler—had just told me the real facts about the structured method. After wavering for years, she finally plunged in with this "easy" method and was using fifty books for two children and schooling for eight to nine hours each day! Others have told me similar stories. I was mentally weeping for all the beginners who had been lead astray by these two words, when Zephi drew me back with a comment about her engineering feat. She had built a dam in the sand.

What is Easy Homeschooling?

Although you will find *Easy Homeschooling* systems throughout this book, here I will highlight its features, especially those not explained elsewhere. In a nutshell—reading aloud produces great results, while using the library saves money. Free and low-cost resources are available; particular techniques and materials encourage excellence.

Easy Homeschoolers learn all the time like unschoolers. We emphasize great books as do those using the Classical method. Reading aloud is a cornerstone, as it is for Charlotte Mason people. We encourage self-study as does Dr. Robinson, and combine subjects as do unit-study enthusiasts. Our students have been accelerated, but without push and shove, without the strain of excess structure. Easy Homeschooling combines the best of the methods with the lowest-cost materials.

Save Money

Easy Homeschooling can save you lots of money. Homeschoolers spend an average of over five hundred dollars each year per child, while some public schools spend as much as eleven thousand dollars!

One year's bottom line for us was only fourteen ($14.00) dollars! True, we have ready access to antique books because we sell them, but we also purchased the expensive Robinson CDs that year. How did we do it? In previous years we bought assorted new items and didn't need them any more so we sold them. But you can save money, even if you have never homeschooled before.

Your tools will include a rich assortment of library books and materials, old and antique books, like-new used materials, leaflets, booklets and art videos. Easy Homeschooling encompasses free or inexpensive do-it-yourself techniques such as how to keep track of high school credits, set up homemaking classes, train your children to draw, and teach math in a unique way.

Save Time

Most of the other methods take much time, as my friend learned in her first year with structured learning. Easy Homeschooling is so time efficient that even a working parent can homeschool! In issue #18 of *Practical Homeschooling* I recommend two or three hours a night and four to five on the weekend. Easy Homeschooling eliminates the "unnecessaries" and focuses on the learning activities that have been proven to give excellent results.

Reading Aloud

"The single most important activity for building the knowledge required for eventual success in reading is reading aloud to children."[1]

Children's success in school is definitely linked to reading skill, which itself springs from early parental involvement. Reading aloud is like leaven that prepares dough for baking. It increases the quality and quantity of brain cells so that a child eventually excels in all educational endeavors, not only in reading. ★ *Reading aloud is the essential activity for all ages.* Do this one thing and you can forget teaching language arts. Your children will begin to read much on their own, acquire a lovely command of the English language and write beautifully. They will use advanced vocabulary, although sometimes mispronounced (a good reason to have your children read aloud, even when older).

✔ *Using the Dictionary.* Most words are understood in context—if they are heard often enough, they will be understood by the way they are used in the sentences. However, it is a good idea to look up unknown words at times when a work—such as a poem—will be reread over several days. Spend a few minutes learning how to understand the symbols that are the key to proper pronunciation and also look up those words that no one knows how to pronounce properly.

What to Read

Read classic works. These authors will garnish your lives with their lovely prose: Beatrix Potter (*Peter Rabbit* and others), Laura Ingalls Wilder (*Little House on the Prairie* and others), Louisa May Alcott (*Little Women, Little Men, Jo's Boys* and others), Charles Dickens (*David Copperfield, The Christmas Carol,* others), and Mark Twain. We laughed all the way through *Tom Sawyer Abroad,* although sometimes Twain's young characters model character one would rather not see in young 'uns! My girls read a lot of James Herriot's books because they love cats. Try authors and poets like Henry Wadsworth Longfellow, Robert Louis Stevenson, John Greenleaf Whittier and

Rudyard Kipling. You don't have to read something just because someone recommends it. If you don't like a work or think it inappropriate for your family, find something better.

Another reason to read aloud—and perhaps even more important than the educational benefit—is to foster family togetherness. You will find that sharing laughter and tears draws your family together.

How to Choose Literature

Don't waste your time on dumbed-down books. Not every book worth reading will have exquisite language, yet after reading a few paragraphs, you will know whether a particular book will foster excellence or mediocrity.

To choose good literature you can rely on catalog descriptions with comments such as "well-written," "interestingly written," "of literary quality" and so forth. If you can see a book, it is even easier to choose literature. Study the following excerpts so that you will be able to choose fine writing. Can you see the superiority of the older selections?

- "Mistress Botsford grabbed a heavy skillet and planted herself firmly in the doorway. If they planned to enter unasked, they'd reckon first with her and her frying pan. The riders drew up. Two of them dismounted. Ten remained on their horses." A *We Were There* book from the 50s
- "Those who returned safely went back to the camp at the valley's entrance. But General Jeffries was not there." A *Signature* book. © 1957

The following are from the 1800s or earlier.
- "During the weeks that elapsed while the three great armies were assembling and taking up their positions, the troops stationed round Brussels had a pleasant time of it." *One of the 28th*, G.A. Henty
- "Graham then gave a brief narration of the direful circumstance. He and his father, Lord Dundaff, having crossed the south coast of Scotland in their way homeward, stopped to rest at Ayr." *Scottish Chiefs*, Jane Porter

- "And having administered this rebuke, as though it were something of a chief importance, he turned to examine our defenses. *Kidnapped,* by R. L. Stevenson
- "The time which passes over our heads so imperceptibly, makes the same gradual change in habits, manners, and character, as in personal appearance. At the revolution of every five years we find ourselves another, and yet the same—there is a change of views, and no less of the light in which we regard them; a change of motives as well as of actions." *The Abbot,* Scott
- "Give every man thine ear, but few thy voice: take each man's censure, but reserve thy judgment." *Hamlet,* Shakespeare
- "Now I beheld in my dream, that they had not journeyed far, but the river and the way for a time parted; at which they were not a little sorry, yet they durst not go out of the way." *Pilgrim's Progress,* Bunyan

The Public Library

Your library has many beautiful and useful books. I was thrilled to find one fragile copy of *Uncle Tom's Cabin* on a bottom shelf in the back of the library. I even asked to purchase it to protect it from the discard pile! We read this title during our Civil War study. I cried more than once while we were reading it. The library has saved us a lot of money—thousands of dollars over the years. I can't imagine where we would put all those books if we had bought them, although we have a large bookcase and several smaller ones throughout our house. Of course you may want to purchase some books for gifts, for reference or for building your own library, but unless you like to be lavish with your financial resources, wait—and in a future chapter, I'll give tips on finding the best books. (Chapter 7, "Enjoying Heirlooms") For school, we select books from the library based on our scope and sequence. (Chapter 5, "Planning for Success") Some years we use mostly nonfiction for science and history. Other years we use more classic literature and biographies.

Learning Materials

Along with books, libraries provide videos, magazines, computers, scanners and printers. Educational software is available. Look for discarded books to purchase. Ask when your library has its annual book sale. We have even had opportunity to attend special homeschoolers' events covering public speaking, crafts, favorite books, science and more.

✓ Foreign language or phonics tapes are available at some libraries. Do an intensive study while you have the program at home. Work until your child wants to stop. Start again after a break. Do as many sessions as possible, forgetting other subjects during this time. Then take the tapes back. Check the program out again in a week or two, and do another intensive study. If you are doing this with a very young child, make sure that he or she is ready for learning and that the program is enjoyable so that burn-out is avoided. Never push! More real progress will be made by letting your child set the pace.

Other Inexpensive or Free Resources

- For the cost of a stamp, you can write to your state government and ask about materials available for educators.
- Are there people in your community—friends or family—who have interesting lifestyles or careers? They might be willing to share their knowledge—perhaps even apprentice your child.
- What can you teach your children that you know? What would you like to learn with your child? Choose from balancing a checkbook, to gardening, to cooking, to any other specialized or ordinary talent that you have or want to learn!
- If you have a friend in a foreign country, ask him to try to find a penpal for your child. Our friend, Ali, from Iran, couldn't find anyone who knew enough English but he did send us a wonderful photograph of ancient Persian ruins!
- Do you know of a foreign college student who would love sharing about his country while enjoying a home-cooked American meal and visit with you?

- Do you have encyclopedias? Teach from them! They are packed with information and if you have an old set, their content will be richer.
- Many free homeschool catalogs have teaching tips included with their product descriptions.
- Your local homeschool support group may have programs available for both you and your child. These will usually be free or low cost.
- Your child could be a volunteer at a living history museum.
- There are many free resources available online—books, courses, outline maps and worksheets. My favorite search engine is ***www.google.com***.

✔ For teachers, the Internet can be quite helpful. For children, let the computer be a glorified typewriter—helping the words flow into wonderful prose. Let the Internet be the fantastic research tool that it is. However, because it is visual, limit time. If you want to accomplish really great things with your children, use books more than the computer.

Teacher Preparation

Good news! With Easy Homeschooling, teacher preparation is unnecessary—other than the occasional books you may wish to read. You save a lot of time. Instead of preparation for "classes," Mom learns along with the kids—as in reading aloud. Mom pursues other interests while the children work independently. I don't even keep a school log or diary, although many recommend it (and some states require it). It just seems like a waste of paper and time and I dislike clutter so I would probably throw it out eventually anyhow! Our children are the "journal" of their education. Once a year, you will design an annual teaching plan (scope and sequence) and a daily schedule. That's it! Then you are free to learn with your children each day. You *may* wish to keep a record of the great books that you read!

Workbooks and Texts

You may choose to use one or two purchased texts or workbooks. Used or antique are fine and less expensive—see "Enjoying Heirlooms," "Resources," or the Internet. These allow your child to work independently which is time-efficient. Some that we have used and can recommend are ☞ *Saxon* math for older students and *Learning Language Arts Through Literature.*

It is very important to have a system of accountability for independent study and the use of workbooks. Check work daily—immediately is best, so that your child can have the satisfaction of having finished the day's work well. Don't allow sloppy work.

Don't forget, you are training for life!

Please don't go out immediately and buy suggested workbooks and texts! Read this whole book first and then you will be better able to decide just what you really need. Take notes. Keep a diary, if you are already homeschooling. See an entire chapter covering several years of our homeschooling experiences in ❀ *Easy Homeschooling Companion,* "Drawing from my Diary."

The Basics and Excellency

Mastery—in the basic subjects of reading, writing and arithmetic—is the keystone of knowledge. These skills are used daily throughout life. In this book, I've shared the easy way to teach the basics. Although a large time investment is not needed to educate well, a concentrated focus during the time that you are schooling will multiply results.

Always follow up if your children are working independently. Drill math facts until they are known and known well. Do not allow calculator use. Require excellence. Attention to these and other suggestions will make the whole process much easier. Decide to be disciplined, even if you have to start with just one thing.

I know from experience how a school can just slide into inactivity, but,unless you are unschooling, it is a mistake. If children know their honest best is expected and shoddy work is not accepted, they will not disappoint you. Be firm for a season and you will be rewarded with diligent children who do excellent work.

Next you will learn how to free up more time for important activities by putting order into your home.

4
Making Order

An undisciplined mom started our homeschool. I tore out paneling—and three years later we were still dining in a kitchen with unpainted plaster walls. I would spend hours, even days, looking through seed catalogs. I had never learned to work. I *should* have been helping more, because my siblings were grown and gone from home, but my parents did everything. Interested in fashion, I spent my pre-adult years looking at fashion magazines. I carried many of these wasteful and irresponsible habits into my adulthood. I became bored quickly with employment, never keeping a job long, and it was very difficult to stay motivated.

When we started schooling, we always had school regularly, but I accomplished little else. Since then I have learned to use lists, plans and schedules to save time and get us to our destination. In this chapter and the next I will explain the same procedures that have helped me fulfill many personal goals as well as homeschool goals. You, too, will soon learn to draft your own blueprint for success!

Organizing Your Home

Our homes are havens for our homeschools. When home is in order, schooling moves forward smoothly. We can make changes in this area in order to free time for homeschooling and for working toward other goals. If things aren't organized and accessible, we not only waste precious time searching but we also destroy inner peace with the frustration of not finding the item(s).

Before starting our business, I organized everything in our house from files to sewing supplies. For years I kept my fabric in a large hinged

box, but every time I would try to find
something, I'd leave things in disorder.
Then we purchased an old wardrobe at an
auction, and my husband fitted it with
shelves for fabric and notions. Shelves in
a closet or even on a wall would work just
as well.

When you get organized, you will
have fewer frustrating moments. We still
have a few areas that get unorganized
quickly, but when I regularly clean and
sort these, upkeep is not overwhelming.

The golden rule for making order out
of chaos is to throw away, give away, put
away. In one word—eliminate! Get rid of
as much as you can do without. I love to
see order emerging in this process. But I
must confess, I have gone overboard in
my quest for order and have later wished I had kept certain things
such as depression glass, pink floral china, antique linens and our
children's toys!

Steps to Order

1) Gather boxes for storage, and a broad-point marker for labeling. I
   like to use additional boxes for trash so I can easily toss items in.
   You could use paper grocery sacks or plastic trash bags as well.
   Check the bags and boxes before disposing of them to be sure you
   do not accidently trash valuables! Always check the bags and boxes
   before disposing of them. We sometimes used large plastic gar-
   bage "cans" and industrial laundry bins on wheels for our discarded
   items. We did not have to empty these containers as often, so they
   were especially helpful in cleaning the second story of our home.
2) Throw away all obvious trash including papers, old mail and catalogs. You will see the beginnings of order and be inspired to continue with your task.

3) Work on one room at a time. As you sort and organize, you will find items that are too good to toss but that you neither want nor need. Put these items in separate boxes to give away or to sell at a garage sale. Label accordingly.

4) Box excess items that you can't bear to part with and label the box.

5) Store these items out of the reach of young children who love to explore. Your bright, inquisitive children can destroy weeks of organizing in minutes!

6) Go through all of your family's clothing, sorting as above. This time make a pile for worn cotton garments. Cut these into one-foot squares for cleaning cloths. If you sew, you may wish to save the buttons from these clothes and reuse them. Use the squares for cleaning, wiping up spills, washing cars, stripping woodwork and so forth. They not only save the cost of paper towels, they usually do a much better job!

8) My mother's maxim is a good one. "Have a place for everything and keep everything in its place." If you don't have a place, make a place.

Cleaning

Once your possessions are organized, you can begin cleaning. This might take a day or even a month if you deep clean everything. I usually vacuum once a week after having one or more of the children pick up. Children should have regular chores, such as keeping their rooms clean and neat, dusting, and washing dishes. For major cleaning, follow the steps below.

Choose a sunny day to clean so you have lots of natural light. Unplug appliances before cleaning them and turn the electricity off at the breaker box before cleaning switches, outlets, and light fixtures. Use a thick rough cloth or sponge, a bucket, warm or hot water, cleaner, a step ladder, an old dish brush, an old toothbrush and a larger floor scrub brush. The brushes will clean cracks, crevices, corners and embossed vinyl flooring. You could make do with just one brush, such as the dish brush. Optional are protective gloves and goggles.

Tackle one room at a time. Kitchens and bathrooms take the most "elbow grease" so start there. In the kitchen, it is best to do the insides of the cupboards, refrigerator and stove before the major cleaning. It might take a day to do the interiors, and another day to do the rest of the kitchen.

Clean each room top to bottom starting with the ceiling. You may wish to use goggles to keep spatters out of your eyes. This cleaning strains lazy muscles, but I prefer washable ceilings. Each room does get easier! Clean the light fixture, then wash the upper walls, cupboards and lower walls. You can clean windows next.

Clean the floor thoroughly. I love my "ugly" Tri-Star® Compact canister vacuum because I can quickly take off the smooth floor attachment and use the metal tube to get into corners and along edges (and even along the ceiling with the brush attachment). Compacts are made well and do a good job, although they are very expensive if purchased new. When you have vacuumed or swept your floor, attack grime with a scrub brush and a strong cleaning solution. Do the baseboards at this time. Change the water often and rinse thoroughly if you want a truly clean floor. There are several all-purpose concentrated products available for washing smooth surfaces, such as Mr. Clean,® Fantastic,® Simple Green® or a generic cleaner from a warehouse store like Sam's Club. A professional cleaning person says, "I use Super Clean® available from Wal-Mart in the auto section—strongest stuff you'll ever see— will take the skin off your fingers! It comes in a gallon and will last a very long time. I dilute it about ten to one to clean almost everything . . . ."[1]

Give a final touch to your floor with a coat or two of wax. Before you know it your house will shine! To make cleaning more manageable, you may choose to do one major cleaning job each week or each month. Once your home is clean and organized, simple daily and weekly upkeep will maintain it. To keep order, pick things up or have your children pick things up immediately when that activity is finished. Have a ten minute daily "pick up" time before or after school. It really doesn't take long to keep your house in order. Letting it go is what makes the job overwhelming!

There are many books available to help you put and keep order in the home, such as those by ☞ **Don Aslett.** You might also wish to access cleaning and organizing resources on the Internet such as *www.flylady.net.*

I told them, "There's no fun like work!"

Delegate

The mutually beneficial relationship that family members share is seldom more evident than in the area of work. Working is an important part of education and one that schooling institutions overlook. A phrase that I coined and use often with my children is: "There's no fun like work!" I love to work because I love to see the results of work: a clean house, a redecorated house, a weed-free garden, knowledgeable children, a quality product and so on. Our children make it possible for us to achieve much more than we could without them. Likewise, our successes and accomplishments are their successes and accomplishments.

✗ Start early with each of your children, let them have some say in what they would like to do and let them know you need them. If you are financially able, pay your children for work well done. Money does motivate, especially if your children are not already overly "blessed." But if you aren't able to pay them, that's fine. They receive their pay with food, clothing, shelter, occasional trips and treats.

Your children will reveal amazing talents. Ezra, when nine, had built a boat and a tool box and was quite handy and helpful, as was our youngest son Eli who even fixed a mower that the repair shop said couldn't be fixed! Zephi liked to change oil in our vehicles.

Schoolroom

We began homeschooling informally so the whole world was our schoolroom. Our van was a schoolroom, as was the river and the backyard. Our couch was our schoolroom, with babes on laps and cuddled nearby. This had to be one of life's most precious times. At that time our couch was directly in front of the bay windows, so we had lots of light. Next, we purchased our "teaching board" (we used a white dry-erase marker board) and wherever that happened to be was our schoolroom. We also used the dining room and kitchen tables.

Our first formal schoolroom was once a junk room. We made order in the room, and it was beautiful, bright, and spic and span. It was a pleasure to be in that room, which made learning a pleasure as well. We decorated it with school things: our white board, a globe, maps and an antique wooden desk. One day the children and I went to an auction at an old school building, and we picked up three more desks for one dollar each!

Next we moved upstairs to our large central hall and covered the walls with a time-line. When we used the hall for other purposes and the first schoolroom became an office, the desks spent some time in our dining room with its floor-to-ceiling bookcase. Sunny bay windows and school decor completed the setting.

The girls then took their individual studies to their rooms. Later they all worked in their rooms at their desks. (I think it is important to check progress often with this approach.)

As long as you do not neglect getting together for family read-aloud times, it really doesn't matter where you do school. I've just shared what we've done to show how flexible "location" can be. However, having a special room adds orderliness because everything is in one place. You spend time on the important things and don't waste it searching for something or moving from room to room. (If you school on

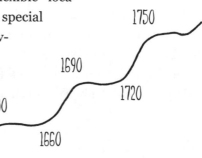

your only table, you must clear it before meals.) It is also easier to supervise your children and their progress if they are in a special room with you or working quietly while you tend to other things.

What about those babies and toddlers? Our solution was simple. We worked on school while they were napping. All of ours took long naps until they were about five or six years old. Older children can work independently while the little ones are awake.

While homeschooling my children, I learned lessons about working and getting organized. Our home became better because of what I learned and implemented.

✗ If possible choose a schoolroom with a southern exposure, especially if you live in a northern state.

Contain Your School
By Marilyn Rockett

Containers are wonderfully useful when you want to organize your school and home, and they are peace treaties between you and your children. When children know exactly where to find their school materials, there is less conflict, and you can spend your valuable time with learning and other important activities. You may not choose to do "school" in just one place in your home, but storing supplies and materials in one place while keeping them portable is usually easier and more efficient. That storage place can be a bookshelf in an accessible place, a cabinet the kids can reach—but you can close when you want a neater look, or low shelves built into a closet. For each student, use a plastic dishpan, marked with the child's name. Inside the pans, put notebooks, schoolbooks, pencils, rulers and any other materials that each child needs. Label the supplies with each child's name, and you will easily see who hasn't cleaned up his or her own mess. These pans are easy to transport wherever you need them. If you use a dining table that you must clear, the pans make it easy and quick for your children to pick up their own things and return them to the storage area.

Another helpful container is a large basket or plastic crate by the back door for anything that must go with you when you leave—library books, items for the support group meeting, dry cleaning, a return to a store and so forth. This prevents your scrambling around looking for the items you need when you plan a trip out. You can even pick up the basket or crate and take it with you to the car.

To keep preschoolers entertained while you work with older children, find a special place for an activity center just for them. Use plastic bins or pans for various materials that suit your preschoolers' interests, containing each activity in a separate pan. Here are some ideas to stimulate your thinking:

- Coloring books, crayons, colored pencils, watercolors
- Blocks and puzzles
- Magnets (letters, numbers) that tell a story. You can make your own by cutting out pictures and gluing a piece of a magnetic strip on the back of each one). Sit the child by the refrigerator to create with his magnets.
- Stickers, rubber stamps with paper, or an "album"
- Play dough (purchased or homemade)
- Pipe cleaners (non-messy fun for children to form and shape to their hearts' content—and they come in many colors)
- Beads (Use a container with a lid for beads or beans). Use the size that is appropriate for the age child and add string on which to string them.
- Use your imagination!

Look for ways to use containers in your home and school for many different purposes. Even a mess looks better when you pile it into a container.

Marilyn Rockett and her husband, Chesley, home educated the younger three of their four sons for fifteen years until their youngest son completed high school studies in 1996. They have six home-taught grandchildren. Marilyn is the author of *Homeschooling at the Speed of Life: Balancing Home, School, and Family in the Real World* (B&H Publishing Group, 2007). She speaks for homeschool events and women's groups. Contact her at *marilyn@MarilynRockett.com*.

www.MarilynRockett.com

5
Planning for Success

I t may be that you struggle to stay motivated. Change for me was a process. Necessity was the catalyst that began that process. I learned procedures along the way that accelerated my ability to get more done in less time and motivated me to accomplish more. In Chapter 1, "Laying Foundations," the concept of recording dreams and goals was introduced. Now we will look into step lists, which are the key to meeting the goals you have set, which in turn will make your dreams come true.

Your Step List

➥ Open your notebook. If you haven't done so, make a separate list of your most important goals. You are now going to make a list of the steps you need to take to reach each of these goals. Start with your short-term goals because short-term goals are often steps to long term goals. For instance, one of my short-term goals is to get organized, which is also a step toward my long-term goal of running a successful business. One of my step lists looks like this:

Goal: Become and Stay Organized
Today's Date_____
Date to be Accomplished_____

1) Get up earlier.
2) Stay up later.
3) Take a time inventory.
4) Make file folders as needed .

5) Sort and discard some clothing.
6) Put things back right after use.
7) Teach kids to do same.
8) Spend ten to fifteen minutes a day picking up.

•• Now list the steps that *you* will take to achieve each of your goals. The steps do not have to be in any particular order. At the left of each step write the date you begin to do it. Then when it becomes a habit or you have accomplished it, note that date on the right side and put one line through the step to cross it off, leaving it readable. It is encouraging to go back and see what you have achieved. You should have one page of steps for each goal. Each step may be simple or more complex—perhaps needing some steps of its own. Later we will detail another helpful tool—the monthly to-do list.

You can school anytime, or all of the time.

Homeschoolers can plan their school year for whatever suits them best. Some choose six weeks on, two weeks off year round. Others school year round with only a few days off. This schedule would make it possible for your child to be finished with his formal schooling at a much younger age or would enable you to spend less time per day on schoolwork. This would be an option for the teaching parent who works full time outside of the home. (See Chapter 12, "Building a Business" for more ideas on how to combine work and homeschooling.)

When our children were younger, I wanted to get outside first thing in the spring to garden. Living in the North, we all wanted to enjoy the warm seasons as much as possible, so we did most of our schooling in the winter when we had to be indoors anyway. I scheduled few hours for spring, summer and fall, and many for winter. Our vacation ran from March or April to September or October, leaving only four or five months for intensive schooling. I knew that I would have to do some serious planning.

Scope and Sequence

"Scope" means *the area covered by a given activity* and "sequence" is defined as *the following of one thing after another*. Simply put, the scope and sequence shows what you plan to cover during your school year, and in what order. You can write your own scope and sequence in outline form with the main headings of language arts, mathematics, social studies (history, geography), health and science. Nebraska required a scope and sequence unless the parent-teacher used a standardized curriculum. (See more on methods in Chapter 11, "Mining Methods and History.") Drafting a scope and sequence may take a bit more effort once a year, but saves time and money throughout the year with better results. Even if your state does not require a scope and sequence, it would be a good idea to do one for your own benefit. You will be able to see at any point during the year what you have covered and what needs to be taught next.

✔ Begin school planning by viewing a curriculum guide such as the simplified ☞ *Course of Study* provided in back of this book. A course of study lists suggested topics for each grade. Pick and choose among topics for a grade level. Don't ever be enslaved by any course of study. If you would rather study a topic or subject that is not on the list, go ahead!

When I wrote my scope and sequence, I attempted to put some order into science and grouped similar topics together. One year we focused on botany, another on chemistry and so on.

In all subject areas, pick what you like from those listed. Look at the grades near your students' grades. If you have children in several different grades, you may combine topics or pick one that all can learn at the same time. I do this frequently with history, science and health. Teach your children who are close in age the same math and language arts. Look through several of the grades and plan ahead to achieve a continuity from year to year.

The following is an idea for a history plan. Again, this is an option only. Your plan will probably be much better! After covering these basics you could go on to English history or the history of another country. You could also study ethnic history, politics or law. Each number below is equivalent to a school year but not necessarily a school grade.

1) World history
2) American history
3) State history

Then, repeating in greater depth or with different emphasis
4) Egyptians, Greeks, Romans, Middle Ages
5) Renaissance
6) American history: explorers to pioneers (including state history)
7) Pioneers to World War II
8) World War II to present

✔ After you have looked over the course of study, begin writing your ☞ **scope and sequence.** I have used the outline format most years. Other years I simply wrote a paragraph about what we were going to study under each subject heading. When writing an outline, your topic headings should be similar, and when using subtopics you should have at least two. For instance under your main heading, "Language Arts," you could have as subtopics, "Reading" and "Writing." Under "Writing" you could list "Themes" and "Poems." Or you

could have all of the different language skills listed equally under your main topic. I often added the heading "Other," with "Music" and "Art" as subtopics. Then below each I listed what type or period of music or art we planned to cover. There may be other subjects or topics that you would like to teach your children. List them also. Make your scope and sequence as simple or as detailed as you like!

Times and Classes

After you have prepared your scope and sequence, you can begin writing your daily schedule. A schedule helps you stay on track and accomplish what needs to be done.

✔ Find the ☞ **Class Schedule Planner** in the back of the book. Enlarge and make several copies or write in pencil. Decide if you want to study a subject in the morning or afternoon. You might choose to start with math or you may decide to do your "together" school—such as reading aloud– first, followed by individual studies such as math. The younger students usually are done before the older ones, so the older ones could continue working on their own after lunch. You can also spend whole days, a week or even a month on one subject or topic. You are the designer! But do plan and schedule, for progress can be haphazard without a plan, just as getting to a destination is often difficult without a road map.

You are the designer of your family school.

To find out how many pages of a workbook or text that your child should do each day:

1) Count the pages or chapters. How many total days do you plan to do school? Let's say your school year is 9 months. Each month has 4 weeks. You have decided to school for 5 days of each week.

2) Multiply to find our how many total days you will be schooling. First multiply 9 times 4 to get a total of 36 weeks. Then multiply 36 x 5 days per week to arrive at 180 days. Your child's penmanship book has 200 pages.

3) Divide 200 by 180 to get 1.11 pages per day. Have your student do one and one half pages per day, which would allow for an occasional missed day. Toward the end of the year, readjust the daily work, perhaps cutting back to one page a day. (Divide the number of pages left by the number of days left.) If 180 days of school are planned and there are only 72 pages in a text, you will know that book or subject will only have to be done about 2 times a week. If

you find that your child needs to do a subject twice a week, choose the days—say Tuesday and Thursday—and enter the subject under those days in the proper time slot. (Science and health are often done only twice a week.)

After you have written a school schedule a few times, it will be easy. Then fill out your planning sheet with whatever times, subjects and intervals you want. You may want to write a note at the bottom or side. I started my chart at 5:00 a.m. one year, because I wanted to list all activities upon arising, such as quiet time and chores.

Your schedule is a tool to help you get more learning done in less time. It is not your master but your slave. Do *not* use it as a weapon. You could use Gayle Graham's idea in *How to Homeschool* and have an alternate schedule for the days you need to stay in bed a little longer. That way you won't be tempted to forget schooling completely on that day. Informal learning—such as reading aloud, library trips, vacations, field trips or other outings—can also be counted as time spent on schooling, so don't fret if you have not spent as much time on task as your schedule says you should.

The Monthly To-Do List

•➤ Look at your step lists and from that make another list. This list will be your monthly to-do list. Only put as much on it as you think can reasonably be accomplished. I have fourteen entries on one month's list. These are things that you will be working on almost every day of the month. These are the most important activities that will bring you the results you want for your life, your children and your family.

If there is something on your list that you do not have completed at the end of the month, transfer that to the next month's list if it is still a priority. When things become routine, it is not necessary to list them. Your list is for projects unique to each day, month, step and goal. Usually your monthly to-do list and your daily list—if you have one—will list an assortment of activities relating to many steps and goals. Here is one of my monthly to-do lists:

1) Start book. Write one chapter.
2) Cover letter to publisher.
3) Learn graphics.
4) Study and apply marketing tools.
5) Make dresses for girls.
6) Write article.
7) Compile media data.
8) Query letter for article.

It is also a good idea to note the date when each activity is accomplished. By regular use of your step list and monthly list you will be spending most of your time on the priorities which will move you toward your goals and dreams.

➥ You can even break your monthly list down into smaller steps. Look at your monthly to-do list, and make yet another list of about six things to do the following day. (If your list is a short one, it is more likely that you will complete it.) This is called the $35,000 List because that's what the president of a large company paid a professional organizer after his staff increased business profits by more than $35,000 after beginning this simple technique.

Motivation for Children

After you have learned how to set goals and have met a number of them, you are qualified to teach this tremendous motivational system to your older children. Give them a permanent notebook with dividers and have them start with their dreams, just as you did. Let them spend a few days or weeks thinking about, and then compiling their dream

Spend your time on what matters most!

list. Then go on and teach them about goals. A goal is a desired effect that can be met within a period of time. Then teach them to compose their goal lists, step lists, monthly lists and daily to-do lists. Emphasize that this is a lifetime project and that their notebook needs to be updated regularly. You may choose to have a "notebook day" once a month until this becomes habitual. As your children see what steps they need to take to meet their goals—and see the progress made by completing these steps—they will take responsibility upon themselves. They will discover that personal initiative produces the results that they want for their lives—just as it does for us.

Have a "notebook day" once a month.

6
Combining Subjects

Have you ever washed dishes while cooking or read while eating? If you have, you have combined tasks. You can also combine subjects to make the most of the time you spend at homeschooling. The following are suggested activities. We did them over several years. Do not try to tackle them all at once. Never neglect the basics to clutter the curriculum with any added activities. The greatest portion of schooling time should be spent reading aloud, and—as your children mature—reading silently. First we will look at how to combine other subjects with history, and then go on to combining in other subject areas.

History

Following the history plan from your scope and sequence or the table of contents from a text, choose books to read aloud. To save money, use your library. We used books from the children's section to introduce a period or country. Historical novels and biographies are even better choices. Your reading will lead to people or events that you will wish to learn more about. Then you can get additional biographies and other more exhaustive books. Combine history with language arts, fine arts, penmanship, home economics, science, travel, geography and speech.

Language Arts

- Dictate some of the more memorable passages from your reading. (For instructions, see upcoming section on spelling.)
- Have your children research a particular aspect of history or a person and write a paper.

Penmanship

- Read history (or science) while your children are doing penmanship or a detailed art lesson. Borrow art videos and other materials about the period you are studying from your public library or from the ☞ **National Gallery of Art.** Purchase inexpensive project booklets on different periods of history from ☞ *Kids Art.* While children are working on art projects, read biographies of artists from the period you are studying.

Fine Arts

- Create a timeline. Get ends of newsprint rolls from your local newspaper. Draw a wavy horizontal line with a wide marker. Label each hill and valley with a year 30 years apart (1630, 1660, etc.), leaving enough space for the events of those thirty years (about 18-24 inches). Have your children draw a picture of each historical figure or event studied with colored markers, including the date of his or her life, or date of event. (Shown is a greatly reduced sample; it was not at an angle.) Ours was very long and we had to put it up along our tall ceilings and over the tops of some door-

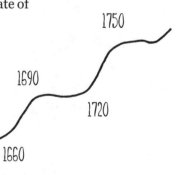

ways. Later we rolled it up for storage.

- Another timeline idea is to use a notebook. Place punched construction paper or poster board into a three-ring binder. Paste pictures cut from magazines, or have your student draw a person or an event from that period and label. You could put each event on one page, with the date at the top of the page, and then put them in order, or you could have one page for each decade. Yes, have your children memorize the most important events and dates.

- Although the above idea is easier to work with, it does not show the full span of history. Perhaps you could do the actual timeline as in the first suggestion, only cutting the time periods into centuries or other divisions so that your timeline is not so long. Then occasionally you could lay it out end to end if you could find room, even outside in the summer on a windless day.

Home Economics

- I have crocheted gift afghans while my girls read, and later they crocheted afghans while I read. You could knit, do needlepoint, embroider or even hem garments during this time.

- One capable child could be cooking or baking while you read.

- You could do crafts from the period, especially valuable home-making or building crafts.

Science

- When studying a period of history, you can veer into scientific topics or personalities. We have done this during our Renaissance study by combining science concepts and the astronomers, da Vinci and Galileo. Your older children could do research and then write a paper.

Travel

- Visit historical sites. Have your children journal about what they have learned. Take photographs or do sketches for a scrapbook to be completed at home.

Geography
- Always look up the place that you are learning about on a map or globe.

Speech
- Have your children read history aloud, practicing the speech skills of enunciation, projection, emphasis and pronunciation.
- Speeches and historical documents—such as the *Gettysburg Address*—can be memorized. Take several days or even weeks to memorize longer passages. Here is how to memorize:

1) Read the complete work together several times.
2) Recite the first sentence together several times.
3) Add another sentence as soon as the first is committed to memory—always reciting all that is known, from the beginning.
4) When you are able to say the entire piece together from memory, start testing your children individually.
5) Once learned, practice often (overlearn), lest it be forgotten.

State History

You can study your state's history using the same combinations mentioned above with free and low-cost materials. Begin planning by contacting your state's government offices. This time, some of those tax dollars will benefit you! Write or call these offices that often have free information or materials.

- Tourism
- Economic Development
- Natural Resources
- Game (wildlife) and Parks
- Historical Society

The Department of Tourism will have an attractive thick magazine that will provide background information, including historical sites and other interesting tidbits. General books about your state, from your library, can be used as an introduction to this study. Read them with your children. Then choose specific areas to focus on. What would you like to know more about? Does your child show an interest in a particular topic? Our boys love to "rough it" and were interested in explorers and cowboys. You might choose native residents, immigrants, exploration or geography. Here is a list of the free or low-cost materials that we used in our state study:

- A booklet of quotes about Crazy Horse. (Native Americans had wonderful memories because their minds were their journals!)
- A man's overview of Nebraska published by the Economic Development Department.
- A booklet describing a particular fort and the daily routines there.
- A free publication called "Trail Tales" published by Game and Parks that features articles on wildlife, endangered species, land areas, nature study and making bird feeders.
- A free newspaper from the historical society. I actually got to pick topics for the six issues and each child received a personal copy.

Combine state history with literature, science, nature study, cultures, the arts, language arts and geography.

Literature
- I wanted to focus on our state's literary heritage, so we read some of our best authors, such as Willa Cather (*My Antonía, O Pioneers!*). Parts of the television version of *My Antonía* were filmed just a few miles from our home. Our living history museum—where more of the movie was filmed—offered a free premiere showing to local residents.

Science

- Although a state study may have history for its hub, other subjects can be studied at the same time. For instance, we took a scientific field trip to an archaeological dig site in our state.

Nature Study, Cultures, The Arts

- Does your coastal state have a large aquarium or other zoo? Is there a special culture in your area that you could study? (Spaniards in California, French in Louisiana, etc.) Has a former or current resident done something notable in art or music? Many populated areas are resource-rich in the arts. Take advantage of this!

Language Arts

- As soon as possible after your field trip, have your child write about the outing, telling what they have learned about their state.

Geography

- Give your children a map while traveling and let them mark your route. Study counties before you go. Passing through the actual area will make the map and the names come alive. Have them draw a map of your state and label each county after they have memorized them. You can also do this with states, or even countries if you are a world traveler or a European citizen. You could use free outline maps from the Internet for this.

A state study can be as open-ended or as focused as you desire. Make it personal and enjoy the time with your family. Mini-vacations visiting your state's sites will foster family togetherness. One of our most memorable state field trips was visiting Chimney Rock and Scottsbluff National Monument, a pioneer passage west. The clouds broke directly over the cliff-like rock formation and a once-in-a-lifetime centennial pony-express rider came by soon after we arrived!

Spelling

If you start reading aloud to your young children, following the suggestions in Chapter 2—teaching one thing at a time and giving your children plenty of opportunity to experience many good books—spelling will not have to be taught. Zephi taught herself to read at five and also taught herself to spell. Seeing an abundance of the printed word, she observed and assimilated proper spelling. Jessica didn't spell quite as well, but she also did not read as well or as much. When I suggested that Jessica become more attentive to how words were spelled in her reading, her spelling also improved.

Our sons have always needed more help. Because of the research done by ☞ Dr. Raymond Moore suggesting that boys mature later than girls, and my own tendency to baby our "babies," I did not expect as much from them. The result was that they did not read as early, nor spell as well and spelling class continued up through high school. I believe greater expectations, at a younger age, would have produced greater results.

Phonics

- If you are going to teach spelling, the perfect time is at the same time you teach phonics because phonics rules are spelling rules!
- A book such as ☞ ***Simply Phonics*** is ideal because it lists the words in families with like sounds and spellings. During each phonics lesson, encourage your child to pay attention to what letters make up each word. Afterwards test orally (or in writing, if they can write). *Simply Phonics* could also be used with an older child who is having difficulty with spelling.

Language Arts

- Copying (copywork) from classic literature is an excellent way to learn language arts, including spelling. Your student reads the selection and copies it. This is easy on the teacher because the proper grammar forms, punctuation, capitalization and spelling are in the selection. Dictation is another effective learning technique. Here's how:

1) Let your students spend some time studying the passage.
2) Read the piece as slowly as necessary for them to get it down.
3) Older children now check (proofread) and edit, marking any errors they think they might have.
4) Teacher checks for grammar, punctuation and spelling mistakes.
5) Make a separate list of misspelled words to look up and correct. (If your children are younger, write the correct spelling for them to learn.)
6) Have your student write each misspelled word about ten times each or speak the spelling aloud.
7) Finally, give an oral or written test.

If your child needs review, he will misspell the word again (and then you will go through the above steps again). To avoid extra work, he will try harder to spell more words correctly and will either learn the words or look them up. To discover your child's grade level in spelling, you can test occasionally using *A Measuring Scale for Ability in Spelling*. Purchase from *www.amazon.com*. You can also use this for spelling lists, if you decide you want your child to learn the most commonly used words.

At least once a week, besides your dictation work, your children should write a story, or other piece. Make sure it's not too long for your younger students. If they are reading independently, they can write about what they have read (this is ideal). Then go on to correct and make a spelling list according to the directions given above for copying and dictation. It is important that your children learn neatness, so it is best that their papers be done in pencil. Otherwise they will have to recopy.

Geography

Combine with research, games, literature and history.

Research
- Make your own calendar or plan, listing one country a week. Have your children do research and report on that country after pointing it out on a world map or globe.

Games
- Play games such as "Where in the World" or "Take Off."

Literature
- Read books such as *Hans Brinker* (The Netherlands). *All Through The Ages* lists books by time periods and geographic regions.

Current Events
- An event in the news can spark a mini-study on a country and its geography.

History
- Geography will be related to historical studies. While studying English history read about England, Ireland, Scotland and Wales. Always find the country that you are reading about on a globe.

Math

Focused Attention

It is so important that parents give their children focused attention. This does not always come easily, even for homeschoolers. Math "class," especially for younger students, is an excellent time for giving this focused attention. Put the baby down for a nap, and send the other children off to work on their own while you spend special time with one of your children. I don't know if I've ever felt closer to our youngest! His smiling brown eyes looked into mine, wondering if his answer was correct. Remember, when it takes a little more time to get them to understand, instead of getting frustrated and short tempered, demonstrate patience and let this be a special time. And be sure to praise them when they get it right

Speech
- Do oral math with your children. Have them speak the problem and solution in complete sentences and with proper diction.

Nature Study

Family Time

Many of us live in beautiful locations where free educational opportunities abound. We spend many pleasant hours in the summer on the sand bars at our river or going on country drives. More than once we have had wonderful nature sightings—deer, bald eagles, hawks, even panther paw prints! Our children certainly can identify more than I could when I was their age! This is an example of learning along with your children.

Drawing, Crafts
- Go outside, open your eyes and *see!*
- Get your children sketchbooks. Sit in a secluded spot (one child at a time works best) and let the richness of nature pour in. Whenever you go on an outing, have a sketching time as part of that outing. Art school students are never without their sketchbooks!
- Check with your state Game and Parks Commission for nature guides for your locality and use them to identify plants and animals.
- Sketch what you are seeing. (Drawing instructions to follow.)
- Label your drawings.

Literature, Language Arts
- Read books like those by Ernest Thompson Seton.
- Have your children keep a nature diary as did the naturalist and writer, John Burroughs.

✔ To make a simple plaster model of animal prints, cut a strip of poster board or other cardboard about one and one-half inches by one foot (depending on size of print). Form it into a ring, and paper-clip together. Push the ring into the soil around the animal print. Mix plaster of Paris according to the directions and pour into the cardboard ring that you have pushed in the soil.

Combining Students

Have older children be responsible for tutoring a sibling. Our youngest son didn't want to begin his first *Saxon* text with me or our eldest daughter. But as soon as twelve-year-old Zephi took over, he did three pages! Even if your older child is not particularly gifted, tutoring will help develop patience and personal skills.

Other Combinations

- Combine vacations with studies by reading about deserts (mountains, the seashore, etc.) before visiting that area and that area's museums.
- Study artists and art history before visiting art museums.
- Study local history and spend a lot of time at local museums.

Our girls attended "school" in an 1890s one-room schoolhouse at our living museum. (This is where I noticed that they were reading better than other homeschoolers their age.)

We have fond recollections of the Civil War re-enactment near "Railroad Town." What beautiful period music, clothing and dancing we savored that balmy summer night! Yet—and importantly—our background reading made it bittersweet, knowing the very real suffering that families experienced during that time.

➻ As you homeschool, you will discover your very own combinations that will save time and make homeschooling easier and more enjoyable! Again, you may choose to write these ideas in your notebook.

7
Enjoying Heirlooms

Growing up in a modern 1950s house with its sterile decor left me reaching back for something fuller and richer. My father worked in a museum and I almost hated to visit—I didn't just want to look at the treasures, I wanted to own them!

Today our priority in dress seems to be comfort whereas in the past it was appearance, including cleanliness, neatness and presentability. Even as recently as the 40s, 50s and into the 60s women wore hats when they did simple activities such as shopping. How wonderfully the Victorians dressed themselves and their houses. Even my grandmother had a beautiful wedding dress—and she lived on the prairie.

Precious People

We have a great treasure in precious older ones. They can share a tremendous amount of history, because they lived it! I am so thankful that our children had a chance to know their grandparents. When we were studying our community, our then seven-year-old daughter interviewed her grandmother. She found out that her great-grandfather was the first rural mail carrier in our area. Later we saw a picture of his "box" on wheels with "U.S. Mail" on the side and a small square opening in front for the reins to pass thorough—keeping out the cold winter winds. Mom told us how he had come to America alone, lived with an uncle for a time and then traveled on to Nebraska.

My father's family lived over the hills in another small community. Uncle Theo, Dad's oldest brother, told how Grandma would bathe, hitch the horses to the buggy and ride over here through the dusty hills. Because she was expecting my father, she came to see Dr. Dickinson, who built, lived in and had his office in the house we have called home for nearly twenty-five years. My two oldest uncles would play on our lawn. How could history be more interesting!

One of our town's oldest residents also shared local history. He's told us about the charm of our tiny community when it was a booming railroad town with livery stables and blacksmith shops. He even told us about incidents in his grandmother's life. When she was a child, Native Americans ransacked their cabin. The motive for this incident became apparent as we read about their very real hunger as natural game was depleted.

✔ Ask your older friends and relatives to tell you and your children about their life when they were younger. General facts can be remembered, but you may want to jot down names and locations. Have your child do a written or oral report after the interview.

"What did you do when you were my age?"

In our studies, we found out that my great-great-grandfather (1829-1924) "had a brilliant mind and at one time was one of the largest landholders in Sherman County"[1] He and his son (1856-1941) came to Nebraska in a covered wagon, taking over a month to get here from Illinois. Great-Great-Grandfather enjoyed splitting wood up to his death at age ninety-six. My mother-in-law said that her grandfather was from Persia (Iran). Even today, there are only a handful of immigrants from the Middle East in our whole state. Those who settled here came from Sweden, Denmark, Germany, Poland, Czechoslovakia and Bohemia.

You too can discover interesting tidbits on your family tree! Visit with family. Check the public library for basic books. Make friends with your reference librarian. Search the Internet. Just as historical studies lead into deeper and deeper studies, genealogical studies can do the same and may become a lifetime hobby.

Skills and Projects

Older people have had years to develop skills. Perhaps they could teach your child something that they do well. How about bartering some home-cooked meals for these "classes"? You would meet a primary need for some of these older people! Let your children help in food preparation. Andy's co-worker could not believe that our little girl had made the bread that he was eating for lunch, nor could he believe that she had been doing it for years. These are skills that other children may not learn until they are adults—I didn't! Homeschooling trains for life.

✔ For a project, adopt a nursing home and go from resident to resident visiting and questioning them about their past. Perhaps you could talk with one resident each visit. Compile your notes into a "book"– each chapter about an individual resident. Most residents have lots of time—but little to do—and would love the company.

Another way to enrich the people in care homes, as well as improving musical talents is to learn *a capella* harmonizing. Get tapes from ☞ *The Lester Family.* On the tapes, the parts are sung separately so they can be learned, and then all parts are sung together. Beautiful!

Heirloom Books

Some people are concerned that antique books will provide outdated information. Consider this: Only 2 percent of recorded history has occurred since 1911![2]

It would be difficult to exhaust the core knowledge found in older books, no matter what the subject. I've found that older books cover the most important topics and ideas more thoroughly and clearly.

To be classified as an antique, an item should be at least fifty years old. In our area, it would be difficult to find a book at a reasonable price and in good condition with a date before 1860. This may be because our state was settled around that time and only a few books were brought with the pioneers. Those that were transported were probably Bibles and copies of *Pilgrim's Progress* that were very used and subsequently worn out before my grandparents were born.

I prefer books with a copyright date from around 1860 to 1930, although newer books with copyright dates into the late 40s can also be delightful. Some books published in the 50s might be acceptable—but not *Dick and Jane* sight readers. Not all books published between these optimal dates are worth buying but they are generally far superior to what you would find today. Another option is to purchase reprinted books such as the 1879 *McGuffey* readers, which can be purchased from ☞ **Home School Treasures.**

In addition to our inventory of ☞ **Exceptional Books,** we have a personal library of old books—acquired throughout the years. When our children were younger, my husband would make a weekly stop at a small library to pick up these "keepers" that the librarian replaced with newer (and often inferior) titles. Some that we acquired during that time were *Kidnapped, The Black Arrow, The Works of Shakespeare, Les Miserables, Treasure Island* and *Little House on the Prairie.*

✗ Look for low-cost, old books at your local thrift store. We found special books at garage sales—such as a poetry book that I had been wanting for years. Auctioneers gave us boxes of books that didn't sell. Even now we occasionally hear of a large number of books that have been trashed because no takers were found. Check with your relatives. Search attics. Buy lower-cost, paperback reprints. Soon you will be able to use the books that you have collected and avoid annual homeschooling expenses and trips to the library, while your children thrive.

There are two basic categories of antique books for the homeschooler—the classic novel and the textbook. The classic novel is sometimes available as an unabridged reprint—but be careful! Some "unabridged" reprints are not the original text, so choose the oldest book you can find rather than a newer copy, whenever possible.

Develop a taste for vintage books.

The antique textbook is not as readily available as a reprint, yet it is a valuable tool. In this category you will find history texts; historical, literary and nature readers; Latin dictionaries and math books.

Other categories are children's novels, biographies and non-fiction. We have an antique set of *The Book of Knowledge* encyclopedias. It is so rich in history, authors, literature, poetry and more, it could be used for your entire curriculum. It even includes a study-guide volume.

For Preschool and Elementary

Do not hesitate to use classic novels to read aloud to your youngest child. Many classics have interesting story lines that your children will follow, especially if yours is a TV- and video-free home.

Continue reading aloud to your elementary-age children. Read aloud from all antique books—history and science textbooks, classic novels, and so forth. Discuss or have your children write about what has been read. Once you start reading aloud, one thing will lead to another. When you find yourself liking a particular poet, look up his biography. Find the author's homeland, state or city on the globe. Then read a book about that place.

Arithmetic

Antique textbooks were written for a child to use and understand so the teacher should have no problem! Many of them include explanatory prefaces and introductions along with answers. They provide problems for young children that are simple enough to check quickly. With the more advanced texts, answers will certainly save time, but you can also use a calculator or have an older child use a calculator or his brain (preferred) to check the work. Teach your children to do exercises very carefully and to always double-check their answers. You may choose to have your child do just a few of the problems presented. This would certainly make checking easier, but make sure that he or she is getting enough practice to be learning.

After two or three years of using ✍ *Practical Arithmetics,* I found that the *Saxon* books were about two levels behind our daughters. We made copies of the pages from the old book and the girls used them like worksheets. The numbers were quite small but they did their figuring on another sheet. Traditionally, the complete problem was copied onto a blackboard or onto notebook paper. You can enlarge the page when you copy it, to use it as a worksheet.

Language Arts

Selections from old poetry books can be memorized and recited. Dictate from them to teach grammar and spelling. Dictate short selections from classic fiction. Dictation is described in detail in Chapter 6, "Combining Subjects," under the heading, Spelling.

After learning to read, our children used *McGuffey's*, the reprinted readers. In the second grade, the girls were at fourth-grade level according to the teacher's guide. I simply had them read to me every day, one lesson at a time. We ignored all the other suggested activities.

Prepare to experience vibrant history.

History

Use an old history text's table of contents for a guide for the history section of your scope and sequence. Read books written at that period of time by someone who lived then, or about that time. If you are introduced to a person you would like to know more about, get a biography from the public library, your personal library or other book source. Do related activities such as studying the art of that period, and even attempting to re-create it. Listen to the music of that epoch in history.

Science

You can do similar studies with science and scientists. Collect scientific biographies, texts, literary works and old experiment books. Combine a biography with books on that scientist's field of research. Re-create his experiment. Write and report.

Proof

Find someone who was educated with these books. Ask the person what they learned in school. You will be amazed at what many of them still remember after fifty or sixty years!

In 1907, Avis Carlson received her eighth-grade diploma. Later in life, she found her examination questions and was surprised at their difficulty: "The questions on that examination in that primitive one-room school, taught by a person who never attended a high school, positively dazed me."[3] Avis was only eleven years old when she exhibited proficiency that today would be beyond exceptional.

Avis graduated from 8th grade when 11!

1907 Education
Home and Health, © 1907, Pacific Press Publishing

A child is recognized as well-educated if he can read distinctly and intelligently, spell correctly, write a smooth, plain hand; and if he acquires a knowledge of the fundamental rules of arithmetic, a fairly good knowledge of the geography of the world and the history of his own country. But if he acquires all the languages, arts and sciences of the schools, without a knowledge of the fundamentals above mentioned, he will forever be set down as an ignorant man.

In selecting a child's reading material, the line should be drawn between the good and the bad. A serious mistake is often made by separating arbitrarily between truth and fiction. ...some imaginative incidents, stories and allegories are the most elevating and beneficial. Parents should select the reading for their children with the utmost care.... Liberal enough provision should be made to keep the children interested in the reading planned for them, so that the active little minds will not reach out with a hungry longing for the worthless story books of their playmates.

One of the most certain ways by which children are led to novel reading is by the negative system of controlling their reading. They are positively forbidden even to look at books of a certain class, but at the same time nothing is provided to satisfy the honest literary hunger of their little hearts.

As soon as the child can begin to comprehend and appreciate what is read to him, he should be led into the most interesting and beneficial literary treasures which can be provided for him. Then when his taste is developed so that he can appreciate and enjoy the good, the true and the beautiful, he will have a bulwark of good taste and principles built up around him . . . .

See Chapter 13, "Sailing Through High School," to find out how to use antique books for high schoolers.

8
The Price of Praise

By Naomi Aldort

When one of my children was about five, he was drawing in an arts and crafts fair. One of the organizers was walking around praising children for their creations. After half an hour or so, she came to me and said, "I don't understand your son. When I praise the other children they smile or show satisfaction or, at least, they thank me. Your son looks blank or just goes on with his art and hardly notices me."

I smiled and said, "He is creating for his own sake and doesn't really care about what anyone else thinks of it. He is doing it for himself. I wish I had this kind of inner freedom and independence."

"I never thought of it that way," she said, "So his confidence comes from inside, without anyone having to say anything. That's powerful."

How many of us act against our own beliefs and even treat our children in ways we don't want to, in an attempt to look right in the eyes of others. How did we learn to need approval? We were trained to be dependent, through praise, rewards and other positive and negative responses to our efforts. Yet, words and actions that intend to make the child feel and do what we want are manipulative and carry the same price as other coercions: loss of intrinsic motivation, loss of self-trust, damaged parent child relationship, lowered self-esteem, dependency, insecurity, disinterest, getting by with as little as possible and more. This does not imply that we become indifferent; on the contrary, when free of the intent to impact the child's actions or behavior, a parent is free to generously and authentically join her child's happiness.

A parent is free to generously and authentically join her child's happiness.

Contrary to common belief, children feel more loved and self-assured when we don't praise them. They remain secure in our unconditional love and free to create their own lives. Instead of learning to live up to expectations, they learn to trust themselves.

As with any manipulation method, the praised child does things for the wrong reason; to get the praise or avoid its absence. As John Holt has said of children, "They are afraid, above all else, of failing, of disappointing or displeasing the many anxious adults around them, whose limitless hopes and expectations for them hang over their heads like a cloud."[1] The only "benefit" of praise is to the adult who gains temporary control over the child.

Sometimes parents say, "But my child looks so happy when I praise him." The happiness we see in the praised child is not pleasure, but rather relief that another pleasing act has been accomplished, securing parental approval (emotional survival) and concealing a feeling of deep loss. Children, too, can be fooled into believing that these pleasing behaviors originate within and have everything to do with who they are. The ultimate deception comes when children grow up to become seemingly accomplished and happy adults. In her book *The Drama of the Gifted Child,* psychoanalyst Alice Miller gives voice to the lamentable conviction that arises: "Without these achievements, these gifts, I could never be loved. . . . Without these qualities, which I have, a person is completely worthless."[2] Miller goes on to explain why achievement based on pleasing denies self-understanding and, in so doing, leads to depression, feelings of "never enough" and other emotional disturbances in even some of the most successful people.

Ways of Nurturing

Nurturing and manipulation contradict each other. To nurture, we can connect with a child by sharing our positive feelings and thoughts in four ways:
- Validation
- Gratitude
- Feedback when requested
- Unconditional love and appreciation

Validation

A child wants to share his success and his joy with us. Instead of trying to manufacture feelings in your child, connect with him by joining his experience or by mirroring the feeling she is already expressing.

Sometimes a child's experience may be different than your idea about it. She may feel disappointed in her creation, embarrassed about her behavior, resentful that she has to do something, or puzzled by the undue fuss and then doubting her own ability to know herself.

A father related to me his early childhood memory of sitting on the top of a big slide contemplating coming down. He sat there for a while and then turned on his belly, feet first. The second he took off his parents cheered and clapped. He was still serious when he arrived at the bottom but not anymore due to contemplation but because he concluded that something was seriously wrong with him or else his parents wouldn't consider it a big deal that he could go down a slide. This conclusion limited him as an adult in many ways.[3]

What could this man's parents have done to express their appreciation without contradicting his inner experience? They could have validated the feeling that was already there, contemplation. After he made it down, they could have waited for him to express his self-satisfaction, and if he did, they could have then joined his joyful expression without exaggerating or dramatizing it. Maybe he would have laughed with delight and they would then laugh with him. Maybe he would have said with a grin on his face, "Did you see me coming down so fast?" They could have smiled and said, "Yes, I saw you sliding fast all the way." They could have asked, "Are you feeling excited?" And yes, if he didn't express anything, it would have been best to say nothing. Later they could have asked him how he liked the playground.

With no intention to generate a feeling in your child, you can simply reflect his joy and join his victory. If your child expresses satisfaction in his art work, you don't evaluate the picture, but mirror the feelings that are already there with a smile or with words. If the child is beaming you can say, "Are you excited about your picture? Would you like to hang it on the wall?" If he is serious, or not satisfied, stay out of the way, or, if he talks, listen to him and show that you understand.

If your child is already conditioned to look for your evaluation and asks, "Is it good, Dad?" You can mirror his need for your approval, "Are you feeling doubtful and do you need to know that I like your picture?" and you can add, "When you ask me to tell you if I like it, I feel concerned because I need to know that you can be pleased with yourself on your own, even if I don't happen to like it." The weaning process can include open discussions on the topic.

In a key note I gave about this topic, a participant said, "I agree with what you are saying, but I will keep praising my son because he beams with joy when I do." Respecting her conclusion, I did not try to change her mind. At lunch time, this mother called me over to her table and said, "Please meet my son." She continued, "I told him what you said, and to my surprise he responded, 'Mom, she is right, please don't praise me any more.'"

Sometimes you may think that your child is asking for praise, yet he isn't. When he says, "look at me" or "listen to my song," follow the instructions. You were not asked to evaluate, nor to "pump" good feelings. Look, listen and give attention.

Even when your child chooses freely to study or to develop a skill, it is better not to praise his endeavor. Let him own his path. When sensing our investment in his path a child may lose his own passion for it. More than once I assist parents whose child stopped his art, sport or music after receiving even one dramatic praise from the adults around him.

Using praise to modify behavior leads to the same difficulties as it does for learning. The child is complying rather than choosing to behave well. Such manipulation builds walls between parent and child because the child perceives the parent as controlling him and not being on his side. When we don't attempt to create a feeling and a behavior in another human being, we can naturally reflect the feelings that are already there.

Gratitude

We want to let a child know that we appreciate her help. Praise is an evaluation and so it misses this intention; anytime we give our opinion or judgment (no matter how great) on the behavior or accomplishment of another, we appear as controlling and as *one up,* which is the reason it is perceived as patronizing. Being patronized diminishes one's view of oneself. In the older child and in adults, such praise is likely to elicit annoyance, shoulder shrug or rolled eyes—because it does not meet the need for respect and equality.

She wishes to know that it served your need or brought you joy.

A mother told me about her twelve-year-old son, who one day, on his own, was mowing the lawn. She praised him, "Oh, how wonderful, you are becoming helpful." The boy stopped mowing. When she asked him why, he said, "When you praise me I know that you are trying to make me do it again, that just kills it for me."

When a child serves your needs she does not want evaluation; she wishes to know that it served your need or brought you joy. The relevant response to the service is gratitude. Say "thank you," or when the service is especially great, express your feeling: If a child surprised you with a ready dinner you can say, "I feel such a relief, now I will be able to enjoy dinner and we will still be on time to the concert."

In a similar way, children want to know that your needs were met when they are being considerate. Praise words like, "You were so nice to stay quiet while I slept," provide evaluation, not gratitude. The children want to know that you have benefitted from their effort. In the case of your afternoon nap you can say, "I feel refreshed and am grateful that you kept quiet. Thank you."

Feedback

Feedback consists of facts, not value judgments. It is not about good or bad but about specific details. Saying, "That was good" tells a student very little because she has no way of assessing what caused the "goodness" and how to improve her performance.

As a parent, give feedback only when you are asked to and only precisely regarding what you have been asked. Adding a "lesson" will most likely generate annoyance, as it is not respectful. If your child does not know yet to request feedback and she asks you if it was good, you can acknowledge, "I feel confused because I don't know what you wish to hear." Ask for direction: "Can you tell me precisely what you need? Would you like me to tell you if your legs were straight?" "Shall I time your run?" "Would you like me to tell you if I hear a note out-of-tune ?" Once you receive a precise instruction, you can provide feedback. To a dancer, "Yes, your legs were straight twice and the back leg was bent on the third leap." To a cellist who asks if his bow changes are smooth, "They were smooth on the first section and bumpy toward the end." If instructed to report your feelings, do not use value words, only feelings: "When I listened to your monologue I felt engaged and toward the end I was moved to tears."

> The child's sense of worth will then not depend on your approval.

The relationship with a teacher is different in only one detail: The teacher need not wait for the student to ask for feedback. By coming to the lesson the child has declared his desire to get feedback and instructions. A teacher can even express general evaluation because it is naturally connected to the specifics that occurred in the lesson; she can say, "I see a great improvement in the quality of your sound," or "I have enjoyed today's practice. Your response to the ball is much quicker now."

While you may feel overwhelmed and wish that you could be more spontaneous, realize that what feels to you like your "real self" is more likely to be a set of habits and old "tapes." While changing such habits, the intention of the heart is by far more important than the perfect wording.

Replacing praise with validation, gratitude and feedback is bound to generate autonomy and self-reliance for your child and a sense of ease for you. The child's sense of worth will then not depend on your approval, nor her achievements, service or behavior but come from within herself—unconditionally. She will then shape her path of learning and growth not as a reaction to what others think, but based in herself.

Unconditional Love and Appreciation

The real "fertilizer" for self-esteem is not praise or rewards, but unconditional expression of love and joy in who your child is. Share your love and admiration with your child in no relation to achievement or behavior. Share whatever is present and real for you at the moment—a smile, a hug, an action or words. Instead of vague expressions of praise share how you feel and how her presence inspires you. While taking a nature walk together you can say, "I feel so happy walking with you. Your interest in nature inspires me." While helping your child wash his hair you can say, "I love washing your hair, I feel so close to you and that is so important to me."

We don't water a flower if it will bloom, we water it so it will bloom.

Giving full attention is one of the loudest ways to express love and recognition of your child's importance in your life. Listen, watch, show interest and cherish her being. If you catch yourself serving her with annoyance, shift to doing so with joy and gratitude. A child who does not have to jump through your hoops to gain love, will feel free to pursue her passions in her own way.

When you don't mean it, don't say it. If your teenager

rolls her eyes or seems annoyed when you say something wonderful about her, you are probably not respectful of her preferences ("not here Mom," or, "not now") or you are dishing out praise instead of expressing unconditional love.

It is when a child behaves in ways that are difficult for us that she need our love and adoration the most. She already doubts herself (even if she hides it well); therefore, she needs to be reminded that your love is not conditional.

I recall when my children and a couple of their friends were having a ball in the bedroom jumping on the bed and laughing. Every now and then I heard screaming. Suddenly the door opened and out came one of my children. He walked over to me: "I disturbed," he started hesitantly, "They said that if I disturb five times I will have to leave the room."

I opened my arms and he climbed into my lap.

"I disturbed five times," he continued.

I kissed and hugged him. I said, "You wanted to stay and play but you couldn't help yourself?"

He nodded.

"I know how hard it can be to control yourself," I validated.

"I know," he said.

I hugged and kissed him again. After a few more validating words he became quiet and I said, "When you tell me what you did, I feel inspired by your honesty." His large eyes shone. I went on, "Sitting together, I feel so connected to you . . . happy to be with you . . . I love everything about the way you are."

"Even when I disturb?" he asked.

"Yes," I responded with a smile. "I love you because you are you." He looked at me and said, "Ah."

He stayed with me for a short while, drinking my unconditional appreciation and love. Then he got up and walked over to play by himself. He looked content and peaceful.

Some parents would wonder whether treating a child so lovingly after he "misbehaved" doesn't "reinforce" the "bad" behavior. However, there is no "bad" behavior in the child, only in our judgmental thoughts. A child does what she does in order to meet her own needs (conscious or not). When we validate her feelings, find out what her needs are, and express our appreciation and love unconditionally, she thrives because she experiences that we care and that she is worthy and loved simply for being herself. The validation of the child's needs does not endorse her actions, it only connects and models kindness. In the process the child learns to recognize the goodness in herself and in others. She learns to look for the unmet needs instead of pointing out what's wrong and she learns the taste of feeling deep connection and love, unconditionally.

Many of us are scared of failing or speaking wrongly because we are so dependent on approval. Without praise for her successes, the child can feel free to fail and come out of it without self-loathing or guilt. Yet, even then, self-doubt may sneak in. This is when your loving appreciation and connection reminds her that she is still the same lovable person.

Words of appreciation, as in the above example, have no evaluation to live up to or to feel confused by. My son, in response, seemed to have felt confident in my love and in knowing that his value in my eyes had not changed. He may have then experienced high self-esteem because being connected increases one's feelings of worth. We all make mistakes and lose control. Give your child the tools to retain his self-appreciation even while making errors.

We don't water a flower if it will bloom, we water it so it will bloom. Love is the water of the human soul. The child who is confident in your love, and her worth, will tap her full potential authentically.

The Emotionally Resilient Teenager

At age fifteen, one of my sons said to me:

> *"I don't understand why adults pretend to be who they are not, in order to be liked. That's a lot of work, and then you are liked for who you are not, so you have to keep pretending."*
>
> *"Don't you try to impress your friends?" I asked.*
>
> *"I want only those friends who love me the way I am," he said.*
>
> *"What about those who tease you?"*
>
> *"It doesn't matter to me," he responded, "I don't need them to like me. The other day Tim came over with two girls and they started teasing and demeaning me. I told them that what they said was fine with me. They continued to put me down and I noticed that it was hard on them that they couldn't hurt me. I just kept saying that it was fine with me what they thought."*

"The only way to be unique is to be you."

> *In another conversation with another of my sons at a similar age, he told me that a friend asked for his advice: "She asked me if she should put an earring in her cheek. She said she wanted to be unique. I said to her, 'Trying to be unique is not unique at all. That's what everyone else does. Everyone tries to be special, using the same fashionable stuff. The only way to be unique is to be you. You are already unique.'"*

Siblings without Schooling

Q: Without school my sons are almost always together and although they often play happily, they also fight and scream at each other a lot. What can I do to ease their relationship?

A: Learning to relate is a lifelong project and most of us eventually die without completing the course. If your sons were in school they would learn one set of relating rules that apply to groups of peers under the control of authorities. In their own family environment they can learn relating skills that are relevant to natural human settings. When witnessing their struggles, we may feel exasperated because we have a need for a peaceful environment and for happy children. We wish that they would use peaceful verbal communication immediately even though we ourselves haven't mastered this skill.

A teenage boy told me that he wished his parents would let him beat up his "annoying" siblings. Yet adults who were hurt by siblings often carry the wounds into adulthood and they wish their parents had assisted them. My suggestion is that you all learn together with equal respect and care for each other. Realizing that you are on a path as a family will help you to be authentic and to cherish the children's process, rather than dread the incidents.

Parents often feel alarmed by their children's dramatic expressions. A father told me how, upon hearing his daughter's screams, he was ready to jump and rescue her from some "horror." Luckily, before he messed things up her brother said, "She keeps these wheels in her box without using them, they are not hers." The girl got excited and as she related her tale of ownership she cracked up at its senselessness. They left together laughing. It isn't always this simple but more often than not all that is needed is a listener.

It is useful for children to solve their own disputes. They learn to relate and to sort out power, feelings and their sense of self. Often our listening is what makes it possible for them to generate those solutions. There are also times when staying uninvolved is not an honest and loving way of relating. Just as you wouldn't leave your two-year old to solve her own problem of crossing the busy street, there are situations between children in which they do appreciate our participation. Intense emotions can cloud the thinking at any age. Empathic listening can dissolve the hard feelings that fuel the discord.

> Avoid taking sides and you will see reduction in your children's struggles.

Allow yourself to be real; children need to experience the impact of their words and actions on others. When you are authentic with them, they learn that "if I raise my voice in distress, or if I hit, someone is going to have feelings about it and may offer assistance." Although you don't want them to learn "the littlest struggle gets my mom all over us," you also don't want them to conclude, "I can scream and no one cares." Authentic expression is not intervention because you don't control the scene. (Even when you take action to stop danger, you need not control the actual dispute.) You can express your feelings, "When I hear you scream, I feel anxious because I imagine that you are being hurt and I want you to be safe." Move away when you are not needed, and when you are, ask validating questions that will assist the child in finding his own needs. Keep reflecting what you hear and be interested rather than wise. Even one word of "advice" seems to erase all the empathic listening and to reignite the rage.

Avoid taking sides and you will see reduction in your children's struggles. You don't wish for a child to think, "If I scream hard my brother will get in trouble." Scolding one child and protecting the other is a way of controlling rather than one of relating. It actually breeds rage, pain and future friction. Instead, empathize with each child fully. Saying to one boy, "I see how angry you feel because you wanted to be first to use the new swing," does not contradict saying to the other child, "You wish your brother would wait his turn patiently." In contrast, if a parent directs with, "Ron, you are older, let Tony be first," and if (in fear and insecurity) Ron follows this direction, he will feel rage and despair. Mom doesn't favor him. At the same time Tony was rescued and will experience himself as powerless. Both children are left with intense feelings that will ignite the next fight.

Rather than preventing struggles, provide tools of compassion and treat children and others with kindness and generosity. Notice their needs. Children often spell out their self-doubt, fears and unmet needs in their treatment of each other. These needs have to be met, and that will then dissolve a lot of the tension. Look for places of stress in your own life, your marriage and your relationship with your children. Most importantly, give each child regular time with you and/or your spouse on his terms, and without his sibling. A child will experience your love and his own worth when one-on-one with you. Feeling secure and content, he is less likely to look for a sense of power in diminishing others.

No home is peaceful at all times and therefore some children's struggles are needed and healthy. Boys in particular are driven by testosterone to exercise aggression with each other. They find their way to peaceful manhood not by emotional repression but by having safe opportunities to practice and to appreciate the benefits of relating in harmony. They need to feel safe to express themselves fully in words, and maybe with the use of a punching bag. Physical activities away from each other can meet both the need to unleash aggression and the need to have a life away from one another.

When we want human behavior to be other than what it is, we suffer. If we replace our resistance with acceptance, perhaps we will be able to celebrate our children's paths of growth and grow with them.
© Copyright Naomi Aldort

☞ **For recommended reading, see "Resources."**

*Naomi Aldor*t is the author of *Raising Our Children, Raising Ourselves*. Parents from around the globe seek Aldort's advice by phone, in person and through her workshops, book and CDs. She guides parents in all issues of parenting, from infants and toddlers through children and teens, as well as the emotional needs of parents. Aldort's guidance is not about gentle ways to control a child, but about a way of being and of understanding a baby/toddler/child/teen so she can be the best of herself, not because she fears you, but because she wants to, of her own free will.

Naomi Aldort's counseling transforms parent-child relationships from reaction and struggle to freedom, power and joy. Her advice columns and articles appear in progressive parenting magazines in the USA, Canada, Australia, United Kingdom and in translations in Israel, Mexico, Holland and Germany. You may read some of her articles on her site. Naomi Aldort is married and a mother of three flourishing young people. To see her youngest, a twelve-year-old musician, visit *www.oliveraldort.com*. For information on phone sessions, to buy the book and CDs and to read articles or register for a free newsletter, visit Naomi at:

www.naomialdort.com

9
Studying Science, Arts & Math

The creative and yet easy methods in this chapter prove that learning really can be fun—and not just for the student! You will learn things you never knew, find novel ways to teach math and even learn to draw!

Science

Believe it or not, science can be learned from books! Not only can you read biographies and autobiographies of famous scientists, you can read literary scientific books. The best are clear and crisp with an underlying enthusiasm for the topic. (See "How to Choose Literature," Chapter 3. What do other educators suggest for science teaching? See Chapter 11.)

Choose one area of science to study each year, such as chemistry, physics, meteorology or biology; or study the science of a period along with its history—according to your scope and sequence. Then go on to read biographies of a scientist who worked in the field you have chosen. Be sure to get the oldest biography possible. Some of the newer books are very poorly written and extremely boring!

You will learn scientific facts from biographies—but to learn more, you can expand your study by checking out scientific books on that topic from the children's or adult's department of your public library.

Finally, you can attempt an experiment in the field that you have read about. The best experiment books have topically divided chapters, so that as you study a scientist you can easily find an appropriate experiment to do. Suggested experiments should have a one-hundred percent success rate and use extremely common materials—those that you are almost sure to have in your home. Several years ago, my husband brought home a library discard that fit those guidelines. It was George Barr's *More Research Ideas for Young Scientist* from the "Young Scientist" series.

We learned about rocket science at a science museum in a bordering state. Another time we explored strobe-light science and other concepts at a nearby museum. More than a day is needed to thoroughly study the topics presented at science museums, so if you have ready access, visit often.

The Scientific Method

✔ You can use the Scientific Method for your experiments, research and nature studies (See Chapter 6). It encompasses:
  • Observation. Look carefully at the specimen being studied.
  • Interpretation. What is happening?
  • Classification. Identify. Find the Latin name.
  • Recording. Sketch and make journal entries.
  • Discovering. Research and study to learn even more.
  • Prediction. What will happen next or in a similar situation?

Art

In third grade, art class consisted of completing the teacher's cookie-cutter projects. My college instructor's idea of art was globs of paint thrown on a canvas. Then I attended Ringling School of Art in Sarasota, Florida where I was introduced to real art training. This was a serious art school. We also had individual classes in color and design, perspective, and still life. The school offered majors in commercial art, fine arts and fashion design.

I also attended Traphagen School of Fashion in New York and fulfilled a childhood dream of learning design and patternmaking. In Hawaii, I did free-lance fashion art for local businesses and worked as an assistant designer. I have done pen and ink drawings, portraits and oil paintings.

With all my art training, I had neglected practice over the years. When I decided to illustrate this book, I found myself with deadlines and other tasks to attend to. Thus the sketches herein were done quickly. Some I like more than others, but all could be done more professionally. I had wanted illustrations in the first edition, so I am thankful that it is finally a reality.

In teaching art to my own children, I was totally inexperienced. Our homeschool's focus was literary, rather than the fine and applied arts. Nevertheless, our children have not had to wait twenty years to get good art training. We began with *Drawing with Children* and our children learned the same basic principles I learned when much older. Of course with the motor skills that they had at two to six years of age, the results were not quite as good. They did well enough, though, to win purple and blue ribbons at our county fair!

Learning to Draw

Learning to draw well is the essence of art training. Although Picasso is remembered for his abstract "cubism," even *he* was trained to draw well and did some absolutely lovely life-like drawings and paintings.

You and your children can learn together in all subjects. Art is no exception. Although art materials traditionally are expensive, you can use copy paper, regular pencils and Crayola® markers from Wal-Mart.

Art class may take more time than other classes, but after you have finished your own work of art, you can read aloud to your children while they are finishing theirs.

An Artist's Eye

The first step in drawing is learning to really see things as they are— developing an artist's "eye." Draw most often from real objects, real people, scenery—sometimes from photographs or other good and simple artwork—but not from memory. Another good reason for drawing from life is to get the proper shading and highlights which are almost impossible to apply correctly otherwise.

Look carefully at your subject, noting such things such as proportion and shape. In art—maybe even more than in other subjects—practice makes perfect! The more you and your children sketch, following these guidelines, the better artists you will be.

What to Look For

Look for the shapes in your subject. Before you put a pencil to the paper, discuss and spend time identifying and discussing the shapes in the scene or still life, and shapes within shapes. Do you see an oval? Perhaps the sky is a big rectangle, behind the circle of leaves and long rectangle of the tree trunk. Some of these won't be so obvious—such as the perfect circle that encloses the upper bodies (arms, head, veil, etc.) in Picasso's *The Lovers*. Practice drawing only the shapes you see, emphasizing their geometry. Monet said it this way:

> *When you go out to paint, try to forget what objects you have before you—a tree, a field, or whatever. Merely think, "Here is a little square of blue, here is an oblong of pink, here a streak of yellow." And paint it just as it looks to you—the exact color and shape . . . .*[1]

Always look for proportions. Check by holding a pencil at arm's length. When sketching a person standing, for instance, check this way. The point of the pencil will be at the top of the head and your thumbnail should be placed on the pencil at the chin line. Holding your thumbnail in position, see how many heads tall the figure is. Then transfer that proportion to your paper. You can do this in checking the proportion of other details too.

A Light Touch

When sketching, always use a light touch. Only darken and add shading when you are sure your composition is the way you want it. When your whole composition is laid down in proper proportions, add deep and dramatic shading, or less shading and more outlining.

Lesson Ideas

1) Practice observing, and then draw only the outlines of the items in your subject.
2) Practice shading evenly. I found that even my best artists needed this practice.
3) On another day, take particular note of the shadows and highlights and put them in—in excess and without outlines. Many of the "masters" emphasized shading and highlighting, which resulted in dramatic and interesting paintings. (See Rembrandt's paintings when doing this lesson.)

Media Choices

When your students are proficient at seeing and sketching, you can go on to different media (materials). Berol Prismacolor® pencils are soft and blend well—if time is taken to shade gradually. We kept them usable for many years by keeping them exclusively for our special art projects. You will need a small inexpensive art pencil sharpener because most sharpeners cut off too much wood and pigment.

Charcoal can be messy. Pastels are colorful and blend easily—but also smear easily. I used Kohinoor Rapidograph® pens in art school but there are now less expensive disposable pens that give equally good results. *Drawing with Children* suggests colored markers. I purchased Crayola® markers but, if at all possible, use art store markers because the discount store markers run and keep your little ones' gorgeous works from being all they could be. They did not prevent our children's works from getting blue and purple ribbons, though!

Mixing Colors

✔ Here's a project for colored pencils or paint (you may use inexpensive watercolor box paints). Observe and match the colors in a subject. Practice with just the primary colors (red, yellow, blue). You will soon know almost instinctively that your grayed blue needs a tiny bit more red to match the violet shadows. Mix your colors on a plastic palette or a Styrofoam® meat tray. When you start easel or on-site painting, you can cut a thumb hole in the meat tray.

Watercolors

The best and easiest watercolor technique I've seen is "Fast and Loose" developed by Ron Ranson.[2]

Mr. Ranson uses few colors, few details, few brushes and very few strokes to produce lovely scenic paintings. You can lean your watercolor pad against a tree, so an easel is not absolutely necessary. My husband built easels for the children one Christmas and painted them in bright primary colors.

How to Paint Scenery

- Go to the scene. Select a good view for your composition. Search out a single dominant feature, but don't put it right in the middle of your paper.
- Using your hake brush (see art supplies below), quickly lay a thin layer of a very pale gray across your sky.
- Rinse your brush (always rinse between colors and change your water often) and mix a blue wash—not too intense, but more intense than the first wash.
- Now again, quickly lay some sky in, leaving white places for clouds—bigger shapes toward the top of your paper and smaller near the horizon (bottom of your sky). Remember, stay quick and loose. Clouds are not distinct ovals, but puffs of imbalanced smoke.

- Now with a gray put in a bit of shading at the bottoms of your clouds. *Isn't that beautiful?!*
- Now put in distant trees in a soft grayed color, again with your hake brush held at an angle and daubed on.
- Stroke on nearby tree roots and bottoms of trunks with the one-inch flat brush or the hake held perpen-

dicularly to the paper. The nearby leaves are daubed on with the hake brush held at an angle.

- Next, the few darker branches that show through the leaves are flipped on with the rigger brush. Lift the tip off quickly making the end of the branch thinner than its base.
- Use a quick flip of your fingernail to cut highlights along these branches (and into rivers and streams as well).
- Waterways are also done "fast and loose." One or two strokes with the flow is all you need. Where different colors of wet paint meets wet, leave a tiny white area to avoid running, but if you do have some running, don't worry about it. That's part of the charm of watercolor painting!
- Put one other darker shading color at the bottom of the trees.
- Make short reflections in the water. Add whatever other shading or small amount of indistinct detail your painting needs, and you are done! Beautiful and easy.

Look for books and videos on Mr. Ranson's method at bookstores, Hobby Lobby or *www.amazon.com*, but check your library first—that's where we got the video *Fast & Loose*.

A similar method can be used with oils paints or acrylics, although these types of paints are worked much more. Because oils dry very slowly and colors usually become muddy if mixed while wet on the canvas, they are better for the studio. There you can work on the painting in stages, letting each step dry over a period of days. Oil is easier to work with than acrylic, in my opinion. I like the blending option and the richer, old-world appearance of the pigments.

Acrylic, although a quick-drying medium, has a somewhat plasticized (exactly what it is) appearance, and colors do not seem to blend as well. Experiment. Get the primary colors and white. (White is not necessary with water colors; just leave the paper blank.) Mix your colors and attempt to paint some simple sketches.

My favorite media—pen, ink & oils

Art Supplies

These are listed in order of importance. Most are available from Hobby Lobby or other art supply stores.

1) *Pencils.* Drawing pencils are graded from B (soft) and H (hard). I prefer a softer pencil with a light touch for initial sketching, then heavier pressure for shading. Choose a harder (lighter) pencil for rough sketching for children who tend to have a naturally heavy hand.

2) *Paper.* Any paper is okay for pencil, but you may wish to purchase a supermarket drawing pad for markers, and watercolor paper for paints. (Ron Ranson suggests 140 pound, 12" x 16" or 16" x 20" sheets for easel painting.)

3) *A kneaded eraser.* Comes in a small block, but should be pulled apart and pushed together (kneaded) often. This eraser is best because it does not damage paper.

4) *Berol Prismacolor pencils.* Available separately or in sets at art supply stores. To save money, instead of a complete set get the primary colors, or greens and browns and blues for nature drawings.

5) *Watercolors.* Mr. Ranson recommends seven colors—raw sienna, ultramarine, lemon yellow, Payne's gray, burnt umber, alazarin crimson and light red.

6) *Brushes.* Mr. Ranson recommends:
   - A two-inch Japanese "Hake" brush.
   - A #3 long haired "rigger."
   - A one-inch flat nylon or man-made brush. This brush is only used for sharp edges, such as buildings and fences.

If these brushes are out of your price range, look—as I did—for similar less expensive brushes. With acrylic and oil paints, you may need other brushes.

7) *Pigments, etc.* Oils (easier to blend), acrylics (faster drying), pastels, drawing pens, ink, and so on.

8) ☞ **Art teaching books.** All the books listed in Resources teach how to draw well, but you may not need a book if you follow the

above instructions and spend a lot of time just drawing. Check your library for art books, history and technique videos, and biographies of artists; search the Internet for drawing tutorials.

Art History

Study history with the art of that period and culture. Pick up big, beautiful art books at your library or borrow ☞ **National Gallery of Art** videos, such as "Old Masters" (Blake, Rembrandt, Goya, etc.), "Modern Masters" (Monet, Cezanne, Renoir, Picasso, Gauguin), and "American Art" (Copley, Cassatt, and some primitive artists).

Making A Musical Flourish
By Cathi-Lyn Dyck

The fastest way to add a rich musical streak to your homeschool is: Just listen to it. It's that simple. The tricky part is getting the radio station or the CD player on track with the program.

With young kids, it's easy to make the music choices. If you're beginning to homeschool with older kids, you may have a bit of a mutiny the first time you put on Beethoven. For that matter, you may not like stepping outside your favorite styles that much yourself.

But it's important to stretch our thinking! Learning is about expanding experience, knowledge and understanding. So here are some suggestions to add music without having to be a maestro.

- Find a radio station that plays classical music. Here in Canada, CBC Radio 2 is a choice resource. Put it on quietly in the background throughout the day. As a kid, I learned to recognize the "signature" sounds of various composers just by regular listening.
- Check online for biographies of famous musicians throughout history and across various cultures. Go to the library and ask about biographical stories suited to your child's age level. Spark interest by watching movies or educational films about these people.

- Find out about ethnic music. Read books about it, look online, and seek out radio that plays it. Weave it into your history or social studies.

- Look on eBay or at secondhand instrument stores for a cheaply-priced glockenspiel. Yes, a glockenspiel. It's a pretty-sounding little instrument kind of like a xylophone. Use it yourself and let the kids experiment with it.

- If you want keyboard skills in your house, but aren't sure about purchasing a piano, look for a keyboard under $200. Make sure you ask for the following: Full-sized keys. Touch-sensitive. Sixty-one-note keyboard. Not much else matters as far as features. If no one takes to it, you have something that will stash in a closet or get bought at your next garage sale, rather than cluttering the living room in a massive way forever and ever.

- Be young yourself. Allow yourself the freedom to toot on a recorder, to try to decode the fingering chart, to make up silly little tunes. Have a funky jam session with a couple of simple instruments. It doesn't have to sound good! It just has to be fun! The main thing is to give your kids great memories of enjoying music with you. This sparks a love in them for the subject, because they love YOU.

- Research online about how to make your own banjo out of an ice cream pail, some fishing line and a bit of board. Or how to make your own kazoo with a comb and some wax paper. Get down on the floor with the baby *and* the older kids, pull out the pots, and play a rhythm game: You tap out a pattern, and they try to copy it. This is exactly the kind of ear training a professional teacher would do. Try and get everyone in the circle to do it in turn. Let everybody takes turns being the "leader."

- Make a habit of humming little tunes and getting the kids to try and copy them. Or, if you're pretty sure you're tone-deaf, play them on the glockenspiel and let the kids imitate. Again, this basic fun is exactly what music teachers do with kids on their instrument of choice.

- Try playing a note and then singing it. (This gets especially hilarious when a whole group tries to sing it together.) Then try playing two notes in a row and singing them both. If you're not sure you're doing it right, play the note at the same time as you sing and see if you can tell whether they match. When I practice singing, I often do this over and over with just a very few notes until I'm sure I've got the correct pitch.

- Buy a set of music flashcards with all the notes and symbols. Make sure it comes with an answer key of some sort so you can figure out what you're looking at. Go to garage sales or second-hand shops and look for music books that say "Beginner" or "Primer" on them. These will have explanations of how the symbols are used, plus examples for the piano. Put together the info from the flashcards and the piano primers. See if you can figure out how to play the tunes on the glockenspiel! Or the recorder!

- If someone really, really wants lessons—or you really want them as part of your homeschool curriculum, see if you can barter with a local musician. Teach a subject for another homeschooler. Let a university student do laundry and have a few meals for free at your house. Share garden produce, housecleaning, dog-walking, or have your kids mow Teacher's lawn and help weed the flowerbeds. This is an especially valuable offer to older people or very busy people—which starving artists do tend to be.

- Don't be afraid! Music is easier than you thought.

Now go turn your radio on!

Cathi-Lyn Dyck is a former unschooled student, visual artist, musician and writer. Also see her chapter, "Thinking Critically." She lives in Manitoba, Canada with her husband and four children. The Dycks have a twenty-five-acre spread where they produce vegetables, natural honey, wild (but not uncultivated) children, original artwork and music, and random helpful writings. You can visit their farm at:

www.mts.net/~lzycre

Math Writing

Although I enjoyed learning math, I had little interest in teaching it. Then I discovered "Math Writing" which combines reading, writing and math. *Perfect!* Students make up stories about individual numbers, read children's books about numbers and learn math concepts by thought, discussion, writing and drawing. Students keep math journals and teachers keep portfolios of the students' math writing. Math writing is a stress-free, easy method!

Marilyn Burns originated math writing in 1975 with ☞ **The I Hate Mathematics! Book.** Past issues of *Instructor* magazine gave me much information.[3] Marilyn says:

> *Writing in math class has two major benefits. It supports students' learning because, in order to get their ideas on paper, children must organize, clarify and reflect on their thinking . . . also benefits teachers . . . writing is a window into what they [the students] understand, how they approach ideas, what misconceptions they harbor and how they feel about what they're discovering.*

When you begin using these methods, Marilyn suggests talking with your students about these reasons for math writing—focusing on the fact that they will be helping *you* by writing in math class. Later, discussion before each session helps the words flow more easily when the child begins to write independently.

"Divide thirteen eggs into four equal parts?"

Technique

Start with one problem such as dividing 13 eggs, 13 candy bars and $13.00 among 4 people. Or have your students examine and write about the difference between two fractions, such as 1/2 and 1/3. After discussion "write a prompt on the board for children to use if they wish. For example: 'I think the answer is_____. I think this because_____.'" This should get them started. Then have them revise and edit so that their writing clearly shows they understand. Encourage them to add detail, telling exactly how they came to their conclusions. Post a list of the different mathematical words you are studying so that it can be referred to when your child is writing. Spelling and grammar can be corrected and a final draft done. Illustrations may be added. Finally, have them read their papers aloud.

To use calculators, have them first do the problem the traditional way and then check with the calculator. Other times your student could first use a calculator and then explain—write and read their papers aloud, telling how they arrived at each solution. "They may write about any idea . . . as long as it makes sense to them and they can explain it." Marilyn says that if the children can explain the process they used to arrive at the answer, they are learning, whether they used a calculator or their brains.

Math Journals

Have your children keep math journals. Tell your students to "include something you learned, you're not sure about or you're wondering about." Marilyn Burns also suggests keeping a portfolio of each child's work. Let the child choose which papers to keep. Have them write about why they chose that particular paper and what they learned in that lesson. Add to their choices your selections—focusing on those that show your child's mathematical thinking skills.

Picture Books

Another literary concept is to check out a picture book from the library that has a number theme and use that as the basis for a math lesson. For example, with a counting book about animals, the lesson could be about finding out how many of each type or color, then how many animals in all, and so forth. Use manipulatives—

even for older children—and let the children use their creativity and individuality. Games can also play a part in this system of math teaching. After the activity, go on and have your children do their math writing about the topic that you have just discussed, book you have just read, game you have just played, problem or solution that your child has just discovered or created.

Philosophy

Marilyn Burns says that we should let the children push the curriculum and not vice-versa. She offers some good advice when she says to focus on depth rather than covering many things lightly. This should be a priority in other subjects as well. Don't allow yourself to be pushed. More real progress will be made if fewer concepts are covered more deeply. And don't eliminate drill! The basic math facts need to be drilled until they are second nature.

Scope & Sequence

To use math writing exclusively as a replacement for workbooks or textbooks, use a guide such as ☞ **Typical Course of Study** to find out which concepts are covered at your child's age. Just don't think you have to do everything in the guide! Your elementary age child has quite a few years to learn, and learn well, the math basics of adding, subtracting, multiplying, dividing, time, money, fractions, story-problems and decimals. Many things are taught that need not be, as they are naturally assimilated by the child over the years. Math writing makes your child comfortable with math concepts and lays a good foundation for mathematical thinking.

You can also use a workbook or textbook. We have used *Saxon* texts with good results. No matter what method or materials you use for math, Marilyn reminds us that partial learning is natural to the learning process. So let's delight in experiencing this process, and not become impatient for the end result!

10

Teaching Writing

—the Easy, Natural Way—

By Janice Campbell

The art of writing has an aura of mystique nearly as intimidating as that surrounding the art of drawing. Many people feel that the ability to write well or to draw accurately stems from innate talent, rather than from a simple learning process. This isn't true, of course. Writing is simply thinking on paper, and a child who is taught to think clearly should be able to write well, just as a person who learns to see accurately can learn to draw well.

The process of teaching writing is actually the process of training the mind to think clearly, and communicate intelligibly. If you want to teach writing, there is a way to do so easily and naturally, as you practice a logical sequence of skills. Remember that the most important ingredient in writing is mental input—primarily reading. All other writing instruction builds on the quality and quantity of reading provided, so good books are the place to begin.

> *Writing—the art of communicating thoughts to the mind, through the eye— is the great invention of the world. Great, very great in enabling us to converse with the dead, the absent, and the unborn, at all distances of time and space; and great not only in its direct benefits, but greatest help to all other inventions.* —Abraham Lincoln (1809-1865)

I have often been asked why students, especially young children, seem to dislike writing assignments. After talking with the parent, I usually find that it is a case of "too much, too soon." Parents often feel that if child can read fluently, he or she should also be able to write fluently. However, reading and writing require different mental processes and motor skills. While reading is primarily a mental process of decoding and comprehending words that have been put together by someone else, writing is much more complex. Not only must the student be able to comprehend words, he must draw upon his own limited knowledge or experience for a subject, organize his thoughts, choose appropriate words (and try to spell them correctly), and use his budding penmanship skills to put it all on paper. It's no wonder that children are overwhelmed by the task!

Readiness

How vain it is to sit down to write when you have not stood up to live! —Henry David Thoreau (1817-1862)

A content-rich life provides material to write about.

It is necessary that children learn to write, but when should they be taught, and how? The timing varies for each child, depending on his mental and physical maturity level and his home life. A child who grows up in a home where books hold a place of honor and television is rarely or never watched will usually be light-years ahead of a child who spends his free time being mindlessly entertained by television or video games. Children who see their parents read and write for pleasure are likely to imitate them at a very young age, thereby increasing their readiness skills.

Parents who spend time in conversation, enjoy a variety of creative pursuits, interact with nature, and read aloud with the family, are providing for their children a content-rich atmosphere and sensory input that will help the children write with vividness, depth, and insight. Laura Ingalls Wilder is a wonderful example of the effectiveness of this "life-style learning." She was able to translate her rich childhood experience into prose that brings that period of history to life. I doubt that she wasted much of her childhood filling out workbooks and answering often-trivial comprehension questions!

Even though life in the twenty-first century is very different from the life recorded in *Little House on the Prairie,* the requirements for developing writing ability are the same for our children as they were for Laura Ingalls Wilder or any other writer:

- Exposure to language and high-quality literature early in life
- Conversation and interaction with adults
- Personal experience with nature
- Time alone for developing thoughts
- Much penmanship practice so that lack of fluency does not limit creative expression.

Ideally, all these things (except penmanship practice) will be part of a child's life from the day he is born.

Reading: The First Step in Writing Instruction

The Six Golden Rules of Writing: Read, read, read, and write, write, write. —Ernest Gaines (1996)

Even if reading and conversation haven't been a regular part of your home life, it's never too late to unplug the television and begin reading aloud and discussing good books with your child. This is the vital first phase of writing instruction—the construction of a sound foundation of literary experience—and ideally it should last from birth through high school, and even beyond, if the family enjoys it. Hearing good literature read aloud does several things:

- It allows the child to hear words put together in a way that is more powerful and expressive than ordinary conversation.
- It exposes the family to vocabulary they may not normally use.
- It often introduces people and places the family would never encounter in real life, opening an opportunity for exploration and understanding of other people and cultures.
- It provides an opportunity to internalize correct grammatical structures in an informal context.
- It often helps to create an atmosphere of emotional intimacy in which personal issues can be discussed in the context of the book's characters and situations.

Reading aloud is foundational, and each family member should have the opportunity to practice the skill. If for some reason it is not possible to do it regularly, at least provide your family with audio books. These can be borrowed from the library, rented, or purchased. Thousands of titles are available, including fiction, biography, poetry, and non-fiction. Audio books usually have the added benefit of being read with perfect diction, which is helpful, not only for understanding, but also for personal pronunciation.

Continued on page 132

Authors and Poets

By Lorraine Curry

These can be read by—or read aloud to—children in older or younger age groups. Most are classics or heirlooms.

1st to 8th Grades

Authors

- Louisa May Alcott: *Little Women* and others.
- James Baldwin: *The Story of Roland, Old Greek Stories*
- Thomas Bulfinch: *The Legends of Charlemagne*
- John Bunyan: *Pilgrims Progress*
- John Burroughs: *Birds and Bees, Sharp Eyes*, other papers
- D.M. Craik (Miss Mulock): *Adventures of a Brownie*
- Charles Dickens: *A Christmas Carol, Pickwick Papers*, others
- Oliver Goldsmith: *The History of Little Goody Two Shoes*
- Nathaniel Hawthorne: *Tanglewood Tales, A Wonder-Book*
- Victor Hugo: *Les Miserables*
- Washington Irving: *The Sketch Book, Tales of a Traveller*, others
- Charles Kingsley: *The Heroes*
- Rudyard Kipling: *The Day's Work, The Jungle Book, Just So Stories*, others
- Jack London: *The Call of the Wild*
- John Muir: *The Boyhood of a Naturalist*
- Helen Nicolay: *The Boy's Life of Ulysses S. Grant*
- Francis Parkman: *The Oregon Trail*
- Beatrix Potter: *Peter Rabbit* and others
- Walter Scott: *Redgauntlet*

- Ernest Thomson Seton: *Animal Heroes, Lives of the Hunted,* others
- William Shakespeare: *A Midsummer Night's Dream*
- Henry van Dyke: *The First Christmas Tree, The Story of the Other Wise Man*
- Kate Douglas Wiggin: *The Birds' Christmas Carol, The Story Hour,* others
- Laura Ingalls Wilder: *Little House on the Prairie,* others
- W.B. Yeats: *The Hourglass* and other plays

Poets

- Katharine Lee Bates: *The Ballad Book*
- William Blake: *Songs of Innocence*
- Robert Browning: *The Pied Piper of Hamelin*
- Lewis Carroll: *Through the Looking Glass*
- H.W. Longfellow: *Collected Poems*
- T.B. Macaulay: *Lays of Ancient Rome*
- Christina Rosetti: *Sing-Song*
- R.L. Stevenson: *A Child's Garden of Verse*
- Alfred Tennyson: *Collected Poems*
- J.G. Whittier: *Collected Poems*

9th to 12th Grades

Basic Documents of American History

Authors

- Dante Alighieri: *The Divine Comedy*
- Aristotle: *Politics and Poetics*
- Austen: *Pride and Prejudice*
- Charlotte Bronte: *Jane Eyre*
- Thomas Bulfinch: *The Age of Fable*
- Cellini: *Autobiography*
- Crane: *The Red Badge of Courage*
- Defoe: *Robinson Crusoe*
- Dickens: *A Tale of Two Cities*
- Emerson: *Essays*

- Benjamin Franklin: *Autobiography*
- Machiavelli: *The Prince*
- Melville: *Moby Dick*
- Milton: *Paradise Lost* and *Paradise Regained*
- Hawthorne: *The House of the Seven Gables*
- Homer: *The Iliad* and *The Odyssey*
- Plato: *The Republic*
- Plutarch: *Lives of Ten Noble Greeks and Romans*
- Scott: *Ivanhoe*
- Shakespeare: *The Complete Tragedies, The Complete Comedies*
- Thoreau: *Walden*
- Tolstoy: *Ann Karenina*
- Twain: *The Adventures of Huckleberry Finn*

Poets

- Francis Bacon
- Robert Browning
- Robert Burns
- Lord Byron
- William Cowper
- Oliver Wendall Holmes
- Ben Jonson
- John Keats
- Charles Lamb
- John Milton
- William Shakespeare
- Percy Bysshe Shelley
- William Wordsworth
- H.W. Longfellow
- Alfred Tennyson
- J.G. Whittier

Continued from page 128

Beyond Reading Aloud: Personal Reading
By Janice Campbell

One thing that the nineteenth century educator, Charlotte Mason, most strongly advocates is that children must learn the habit of personal reading. She writes, "This habit should be begun early; so soon as the child can read at all, he should read for himself, and to himself, history, legends, fairy tales, and other suitable matter."[1] It is not enough that a child reads, however. He or she must learn to read well in order to prepare for future narration and writing. Miss Mason goes on to say, "He should be trained from the first to think that one reading of any lesson is enough to enable him to narrate what he has read, and will thus get the habit of slow, careful reading, intelligent even when it is silent, because he reads with an eye to the full meaning of every clause."[2] This sort of reading is like gentle watering—it sinks deep into the thirsty mind of the child, providing nourishment for the imagination and food for thought.

Build Skills Through Copying and Narration

We are what we write. —Michael Wood (1995)

Most children launch naturally into the second phase of writing instruction with very little prompting from the parent. Fingers clenched around a fat pencil, they work hard to copy the letters of their name, or a title for the drawing they have just created. At this stage, you will often hear, "Mommy, can you write [something] for me?" as they realize that letters put together in a certain order mean something. This is also the stage when they will want to re-tell (often at great length) a story you have read or they have heard on tape. Copying and re-telling, often called narration, are critical to the development of writing skills, as they develop many of the mental processes necessary to good writing.

Copying

True ease in writing comes from art, not chance, As those who move easiest who have learn'd to dance. — Alexander Pope (1688-1744)

The importance of copying is often underestimated, and it is discarded as soon as a child is able to write a few words on his own. This is unfortunate, for frequent copying of well-written sentences or paragraphs provides several benefits:

True ease in writing comes from art. — Pope

- The opportunity to see and re-produce properly written and punctuated writing many times before attempting to do it independently
- The opportunity to become familiar with new words in a low-stress learning situation
- Practice in handwriting without the distraction of trying to create content and remember how to format, spell, and punctuate it
- Multi-sensory input tends to be memorable. If a child sees a word written, says the word himself as he writes it, he has engaged several senses, and is likely to internalize the information after following the process over time.

The easiest way to approach copying is to use a piece of child's lined paper—I like the size of the lined paper designed for third and fourth graders—and write a sentence, verse, or quotation, using the style of printing you are teaching your child. Skip a line between each line that you write, so that the child can form his letters directly beneath yours. This is much more practical than simply writing line after line of the same letter. It allows the child to see and copy proper letter and word spacing as well as proper letter formation, capitalization, and punctuation. Do this daily until the child is able to copy neatly and easily—a stage that girls seem to reach earlier than boys.

If you want your children to learn italic writing, a beautiful and natural style, you can either learn it yourself in order to make the copy masters, or you can use a handwriting program such as *Fluent Handwriting* by Nan Jay Barchowsky. The logical, easy-to-use textbook is accompanied by a CD with installable fonts for the beautiful Barchowsky writing. It's fast and efficient to type in double-spaced text for your copy sheet, using a point size that is manageable for your child, and then print out as many copies as needed.

Narration

Writing and speaking, when carefully performed, may be reciprocally beneficial, as it appears that by writing we speak with great accuracy, and by speaking we write with great ease. —Quintillion (circa A.D. 35-100)

During this stage of learning, you can use narration to begin working on the writing readiness skills of thought organization and sequencing. Read a story to your child and have him re-tell or narrate it back to you in sequence. Charlotte Mason, the nineteenth-century educator whose classical methods have been adapted for homeschooling by Susan Schaeffer Macaulay, Penny Gardner, and Karen Andreola, used retelling as a major learning tool and a means of evaluation. As the child listens to a story, he selects those parts that seem the most important, mentally organizes them, and chooses the words with which to narrate the story back.

Speaking is oral composition.

Just as writing helps an adult or older student detect gaps in his or her knowledge, narration helps younger students discover their strengths and weaknesses in listening and comprehension. Narration also allows the teacher to immediately detect and correct comprehension problems. Once a child has mastered the skills required for verbal narration, he will find it much easier to move into written narration than a child who has never had to organize and focus his thoughts in order to convey specific meaning.

Suggestions for Spelling

Illiterate spelling is usually a sign of sparse reading. —Charlotte Mason

Although many people believe that the ability to spell well is something that a student is either born with, or not, Charlotte Mason believed that "the gift of spelling depends upon the power the eye possesses to 'take' (in a photographic sense) a detailed picture of a word; and this is a power and habit which must be cultivated in children from the first."[3] My experience indicates this is true. Visual learners seem to spell more easily than auditory or kinesthetic learners, but each type of learner can gain enough skill to avoid disgracing himself if writing without the benefit of spell-check.

A child who reads often tends to spell well, so personal reading time can be considered an important part of learning to spelll. In teaching my own boys, I never found it useful to have a separate spelling curriculum. We simply followed Miss Mason's instructions for dictation, allowing time for visualization of difficult words, focusing on preventing mistakes, rather than correcting them after they occur, and quickly erasing those that slip by. Miss Mason states that "once the eye sees a misspelt word, that image remains; and if there is also the image of the word rightly spelt, we are perplexed as to which is which."[4]

Beyond these simple principles, I would suggest that the study of Latin will greatly improve spelling, along with vocabulary, organization of thought, and other writing skills. Although I don't have space to cover all the reasons here, I suggest reading *The Latin Centered Curriculum* by Andrew Campbell (no relation to me) in order to understand what Latin will do for your student's writing and thinking abilities.

Dictation Sharpens Writing Mechanics

When the child has gained skill in copying and narration, it is time to begin working with dictation. If you prefer to work with carefully planned and sequenced lessons, there are several good writing curricula such as *Imitations in Writing* and *Learning Language Arts Through Literature* that use dictation as a foundation. Otherwise, you can simply choose a brief verse, rhyme, or quotation from a good book and dictate it to the child.

As she makes clear in her book, *Home Education,* Charlotte Mason does not suggest using dictation as a test of skills, but rather as a teaching tool. The passage to be dictated is not sprung on the student without preparation—instead, the student first studies the passage in order to see the correct spelling of difficult words and the mechanics of punctuation.

Once the student has looked carefully at the passage, visualizing the shape and appearance of unfamiliar words, dictation begins. Miss Mason offers detailed instructions for the process: ". . . the teacher gives out the dictation, clause by clause, each clause repeated once. She dictates with a view to the pointing [punctuation], which the children are expected to put in as they write; but they must not be told 'comma,' 'semicolon,' etc."[5]

Allow the student plenty of time to write, then go over the paper with him, helping him to evaluate and correct the piece. You may be shocked to discover that the neat, careful handwriting the child has developed over the past few months of copying has almost completely disappeared! As the child turns his attention to capturing on paper words he cannot see, he will be distracted from his former focus on careful letter formation. Don't be alarmed—this is normal and with encouragement and practice will soon correct itself.

Continue practice with dictation, increasing the length and difficulty of the dictation pieces until you feel that the child has mastered the skills involved. Charlotte Mason suggests that "a child of eight or nine prepares a paragraph, older children a page, or two or three pages."[6] I have even found that dictation can be useful for high school students in helping to start the flow of ideas when preparing to analyze a piece of literature. If the student is analyzing a passage from Dante's *Inferno,* for example, dictate the passage to him. The act of writing down the words while hearing them read can act as a powerful, multisensory learning tool, and when the student looks at the words once again, he will often find his mind bubbling with new ideas and fresh understanding.

Dictate to older students to jump-start their creativity.

Once the younger student is comfortable with dictation, he will be able to use writing as a means of communication, not only in birthday lists and captions for his drawings, but also for letters and stories. If you would like to provide supplemental practice in recognizing and correcting errors in punctuation and grammar, the *Great Editing Adventure* and the *Editor-in-Chief* workbooks are good resources.

Composition: Creative and Expository Writing

Next to the doing of things that deserve to be written, there is nothing that gets a man more credit, or gives him more pleasure than to write things that deserve to be read. —Pliny the Younger (circa A.D. 62-113)

Composition pulls the previous skills together.

The essence of writing is to know your subject. —David McCullough (1933-)

Once your child has achieved fluency in copying (penmanship and visualization of correctly written passages), narration (mental organization, sequencing, word choice), and dictation (spelling, punctuation, proof-reading), he is ready to add the skill of composition. This is the writing stage in which the student pulls together all the skills he or she has learned, and applies them to either creative or expository writing.

Creative writing, which includes the composition of poetry, stories, and personal essays, often seems to come more easily to girls than to boys. While enjoyable, it is a skill that has limited use in the adult world, except for a talented few who will become published writers. Expository writing, on the other hand, is useful in many situations throughout life. Expository writing includes reports and articles, descriptive, informative, and persuasive essays, and other non-fiction writing. The composition stage begins earlier for some children than for others, but most students are ready to begin sometime in the middle grades. There are several points to remember when teaching the composition stage of writing:

- It is not a speedy process—a completed composition sequence includes establishing a topic, gathering and organizing information, creating a rough draft, evaluating and improving the rough draft, and presentation of a final draft.
- Much of the writing process is mental—allow time for brainstorming and mental organization of ideas.
- Work with the student's natural learning style—some students enjoy visual organizing methods such as mind maps, others like

the structure of an outline, and some prefer to do most of the pre-writing process mentally.

- It is not necessary to go through the entire composition sequence with every assignment, particularly if the student is writing frequently for other class work.

- Integrate writing lessons with other subjects by using the composition sequence for history, literature, or science topics.

- Early composition assignments should be brief—don't spring a five-page essay assignment on a student who is accustomed to dictation of no more than a page at a time.

- The writing process can be made less painful for reluctant writers by permitting them to choose topics they find interesting.

- A rich vocabulary is best developed through reading good literature, but extra instruction can be useful. *Vocabulary from Classical Roots* is my favorite of the available vocabulary workbooks series.

First Steps in Composition: The Ben Franklin Method

There are many textbooks available for teaching composition, but it is possible for a motivated student to become an excellent writer using what I call the "Ben Franklin method." In *The Autobiography of Benjamin Franklin,* Franklin relates how, after his father pointed out his lack of "elegance of expression," he taught himself to write more elegantly and expressively:

> *About this time I met with an odd volume of the Spectator—I thought the writing excellent, and wished, if possible, to imitate it. With this view I took some of the papers, and, making short hints of the sentiment in each sentence laid them by a few days, and then, without looking at the book, try'd to compleat the papers again, by expressing each hinted sentiment at length, and as fully as it had been expressed before, in any suitable words that should come hand. Then I com-*

pared my Spectator with the original, discovered some of my faults, and corrected them. But I found I wanted a stock of words, or a readiness in recollecting and using them. Therefore I took some of the tales and turned then into verse; and, after a time, when I had pretty well forgotten the prose, turned them back again. I also sometimes jumbled my collections of hints into confusion, and after some weeks endeavored to reduce them into the best order, before I began to form the full sentences and compleat the paper. This was to teach me method in the arrangement of thoughts. By comparing my work afterwards with the original, I discovered many faults and amended them; but I sometimes had the pleasure of fancying that, in certain particulars of small import, I had been lucky enough to improve the method or the language.[7]

Franklin apparently pursued his self-education in writing during his early teens, and this is a reasonable age for students with a strong foundation in reading and dictation to begin working with more challenging assignments.

Beyond Ben Franklin: Creating Writing Assignments

Once the student has mastered Ben Franklin's technique of transforming the ideas of others into new compositions, it is time to begin creating compositions from the ground up. My favorite writing assignments focus on literary analysis for a number of reasons. First, by the time students reach this point in learning to write, they will be accomplished readers. Thus, literature is a familiar friend, and they can approach writing about books with less trepidation than if they are writing about something unfamiliar. Second, great literature is laden with ideas, and digging through it to uncover hidden treasure is immensely rewarding. Third, literary analysis encourages deep, critical thinking about important issues, so students feel they are writing about things that truly matter. And finally, reading great books is challenging but fun, and everyone should do at least a bit of it!

When I am planning a high-school writing assignment, I prefer to work with literature that has stood the test of time. This usually means the kind of books that used to appear on high school reading lists across the country. The older books are really the best. Most of them are so interwoven into our culture that reading them unlocks countless allusions that crop up in everything from newspaper articles to blogs to advertising. When your student comes across a reference to someone who "works like Tom Sawyer paints his fence," will she understand that the person in question gets other people to pay him to do the work he is supposed to do, or will the allusion entirely escape her? If she reads the old stuff, she will understand much more of what she reads, every day of her life.

Reading older books unlocks countless allusions.

A well-constructed writing assignment will be narrow enough to cause the student to focus deeply on an issue in the text that is being considered, but it will also be broad enough to allow for the possibility of differing interpretations. The best way to present an assignment is usually in the form an essay question. Here is a sample question for the analysis of a passage in *Wuthering Heights* by Emily Bronte:

In Wuthering Heights, Bronte works with pairs. In a 750-word essay, consider her intention, and the effect of twos: Wuthering Heights and Thrushcross Grange; two families, each with two children; two couples (Catherine and Edgar, and Heathcliff and Isabella); two narrators; the doubling up of names. —Zeitgist Literature English IV: British Literature *(see source at end of chapter).*

If you look at the information in the question, you will see specific guidelines for the student's essay. He or she will not be simply writing a book report, but will be analyzing the author's intention and technique, along with the meaning conveyed by the use of this particular literary device. The length of the essay, 750 words, provides enough room for the student to consider each aspect of the question without becoming wordy or vague.

A sample question for poetry analysis is slightly different. It usually involves analysis of the imagery in the poem, as well as the poetic structure. Here is a sample question for the analysis of "The Windhover" by Gerard Manley Hopkins:

> *Make a close reading of "The Windhover" by Gerard Manley Hopkins. In a 600-word essay, discuss how the images and figurative language in the poem complement one another. Show also how the poet uses sound, including consonance, assonance, and rhyme, in constructing his poetic argument. Consider also how he develops his poetic argument from the beginning to the end of his poem.* —Zeitgist Literature English IV: British Literature

Can you see how a question like this provides specific direction for the analysis? If you were to simply tell the student to analyze the poem, it would be impossible to accomplish in 600 words. You would end up with an essay full of bland generalities, and very few specifics. The question narrows the topic, and makes the essay possible to write and to evaluate. If you find it difficult to come up with questions on your own, you may use a pre-packaged curriculum that includes study questions, such as my own *Zeitgeist Literature* courses, or you may simply use questions found in study guides such as *Cliff Notes* or *Spark Notes*. Whatever you choose, remember that a poorly designed assignment usually results in a low-quality essay, so be sure to spend the time needed to create or find well-constructed assignments

Evaluating Writing

Vigorous writing is concise. A sentence should contain no unnecessary words, a paragraph no unnecessary sentences, for the same reason that a drawing should have no unnecessary lines and a machine no unnecessary parts. This requires not that the writer make all his sentences short, or that he avoid all detail and treat his subjects only in outline, but that every word tell. —William Strunk, Jr. (1869-1946), *The Elements of Style.*

The evaluation process is very important in helping the student learn to write. Ben Franklin apparently evaluated his own writing, using published writing as a standard of comparison. I would not expect most students to be motivated enough to do that, but parents can learn to evaluate by reading extensively. If you are not comfortable with your skill in evaluation, you may be able to find another homeschool mom or a friendly English major to evaluate your student's work and provide feedback. You can also seize the opportunity to improve your own skills, and learn to discern good writing by reading books such as *On Writing Well* by William Zinsser or *Elements of Style* by William Strunk and E.B. White. Writing is the most permanent form of communication, and when you take the time to improve your own skills, you demonstrate to your students that you believe writing is important.

✔ One of the best things you can do for your student is to use a rubric to evaluate writing. I suggest using the 6-Traits rubric which offers guides for evaluating student writing in the following six areas: Ideas and Content; Organization; Voice; Word Choice; Sentence Fluency; and Conventions. The 6-Traits rubric provides objective standards in each of the six listed areas. For each writing assignment, you read your student's work, evaluating each area as you go. I use plus, equals, and minus symbols beside each trait to indicate how well I think the student has performed. If he or she has exceeded expectations, I award a plus. If expectations are met, an equal sign; and if the trait needs more work, a minus sign. This allows the student to see exactly what he or she needs to work on in the next assignment.You can find a detailed assessment model at the link below. If this link has changed by the time you read this book, please visit my website (end of chapter) for an updated link.

www.nwrel.org/assessment/toolkit/98/traits/index.html

Coming Full Circle

Finally, remember that the process of teaching writing does not begin with composition, but with reading. Without adequate input, a student cannot be expected to produce quality output. In order to avoid frustrating students and causing them to feel that they hate writing, you must provide plenty of information in the form of books to read, plenty of practice with the mechanical skills of copying, narration, and dictation, and plenty of time for the development and organization of ideas. It is just as difficult to wring water from a dry sponge as it is to extract meaningful writing from a child who has not been saturated in the written word. As a homeschool parent, you have the opportunity to gently shepherd your child into a world of literary delight, so relax and enjoy the process. You can do it!

© 2006 by Janice Campbell.

Janice Campbell is an alternative education specialist, writer, and speaker, and the author of *Transcripts Made Easy: Your Friendly Guide to High School Paperwork, Get a Jump Start on College! A Practical Guide for Teens,* and the *Zeitgeist Literature* series. For more articles and resources to help you homeschool through high school and beyond, visit her website at:

www. EverydayEducation.com

11
Mining Methods & History

Each educational philosophy and method has something to offer. In this chapter we mine nuggets of "gold" from a few methods and historical philosophies that are compatible with Easy Homeschooling. If you would like to know more about the topics in this chapter, see "Resources" or *Easy Homeschooling Companion* or do an Internet search.

The Greeks

Some consider Greek culture the epitome of learning, knowledge, art, wisdom and democracy. Yet, with the Greeks, the State appears distinctly and avowedly the educator.

At Sparta, training for military strength was foremost, while in Athens, the training of the mind prevailed. At the age of seven, a teacher—usually a slave—was charged with the oversight of the child. The pupil attended schools from sunrise to sunset and studied grammar, physical education and music. Arithmetic was elementary. Later, drawing, geometry and geography were added to the curriculum. The students were also taught to sing and play stringed instruments. "Music," Aristotle said, "brings harmony." For reading, they first learned letters, and then spelled easy syllables and words. When sufficiently skilled in this, the teacher dictated portions of poems. Homer was used to teach history, reading and mythology.

Socrates

Socrates taught through questioning that compelled his students to form clear ideas. His purpose was to convince men of their errors and in so doing to confound their arrogance. He also hoped, by this questioning, to teach truth. Two types of questions were used by Socrates:

1) *Ironical questions convinced of error.* A man was led on step by step until, suddenly and unexpectedly, he was brought face to face with the logical consequences of his opinion. This method either convinced him of his error or rendered him unable to maintain it with argument.

2) *Maieutic or birth-giving questions developed a fundamental truth.* Men, whose opinions or purposes in life were not yet clearly formed, were questioned as in ironical questioning.

The Romans

Rome's tremendous power resulted from the home life that prevailed until wealth and luxury began their corrupting influences. There was a freedom and dignity vested in Roman motherhood, resulting in home influences which were both powerful and ennobling.

It seems to have been quite common for girls as well as boys to attend elementary schools. The first schools were military and religious. Students recited a "catechism" containing the names of the gods and goddesses, and studied the Twelve Tables (law). The fruit of this education was robust, courageous, disciplined and very patriotic citizens. The virtues of Rome were the result of:

- Firm family discipline, with strong authority
- The high esteem of the mother's position as guardian of the family circle and the teacher of her children
- A regularity and exactness of the most ordinary acts of daily life, which was the result of their religion

Rome conquered Greece, and then Greek ideas—including their ideas of education—conquered Rome. The children were then entrusted to a pedagogue, whose faults and vices were overlooked. The slave who was a drunkard or glutton—unfit for any other work—was placed over the children as teacher. But the Romans never considered education as a duty of the State. "Our ancestors," said Cicero, "did not wish that children should be educated by fixed rules, determined by the laws, publicly promulgated and made uniform for all."

The Trivium

1) Nine- to eleven-year-olds should be taught demanding memory work—their strength. "Let study be to him a play; ask him questions; commend him when he does well; and . . . let him enjoy the consciousness of his little gains in wisdom." Writing practice should contain, "not senseless maxims, but moral truths." Quintillion did not counsel haste in any case. "We can scarcely believe how progress in reading is retarded by attempting to go too fast."
2) As soon as the child could read and write (twelve to fourteen) he was taught grammar and rhetoric. Composition and narratives accompanied the study of the rules of grammar. At this time, geometry, music and philosophy were also studied. All of these, according to Quintillion, were instruments for an education in oratory.
3) At fourteen to sixteen, the child was to begin to study philosophy, physics or the science of nature, and morals—all of which furnish the orator with ideas—and logic, which teaches him the art of distributing them in a consecutive line of argument. He also learned geometry as a discipline of the mind and music to cultivate a sense of harmony.

Seneca said, "We should learn, not for the sake of school, but for the purposes of life," *non scholœ, sed vitœ discimus.* He also criticized confused and ill-directed reading that does not enrich the understanding and recommended the profound study of a single book, *timeo hominem unius libri.* He said that the best way of being taught is to teach, *docendo discimus,* and that "the end is attained sooner by example than by precept," *longum iter per præcepta, breve per exempla*. The history of Rome proves that the best educator is the family.

☞ Classical Homeschooling

The aim of classical education is that the individual use language effectively and persuasively. Classical education emphasizes Latin, logic and rhetoric.

A genuinely classical education

> *assumed an environment bursting with language, in stark contrast to our own more image-centered day. The classical mind was a mind surrounded by an ocean of language. Every day, all day, in work, education, recreation, church and civil duties—language, as opposed to communication by images, governed experience . . . [and] produced minds and habits very different from those of a culture like our own.*[1]

Language requires precise mental discipline (thought), whereas the visual promotes idle minds. Only mental discipline, acquired by literary learning, results in growth, intelligence and maturation—obviously lacking from many in an image-centered culture. For a truly classical mind, language should far surpass time spent with images. (Even fine art should be subordinate.)

> *Most homeschoolers have an obvious aversion to television, but by regularly providing their children with cartoons and video games, [they] do nothing to encourage the habits of reading . . . [however] a classical perspective in education gives us a reprieve from such frenzy (entertainment, entertainment, entertainment). It reminds us to slow down, to read carefully, to meditate calmly, to work honorably.*[2]

Classical education is more than just adding Latin or Greek to one's curriculum. Parents should educate simply for mastery in the basics of writing, reading and speaking. They should not complicate education with every course available nor should they be concerned with entertaining children.

Classical education is about literature, history, languages and math. Abstract thinking in arithmetic and counting is important. A child does not need manipulatives. "Science . . . should be taught under the aegis of literature and history—we should read the great words of the great scientists."[3]

Not hard work, but discipline and attention.

Hard Work

It is said that the classical method takes "hard work." We all know that "reading" isn't hard work, but to take up a book and read takes discipline; to comprehend, takes attention. Beyond much reading—and more important—is quality reading. Although a purpose of classical education is to teach children to learn for themselves, this curriculum also says that children need to be taught, or led to an understanding, and that children cannot be taught literature that the parents have not read.

Classical education conducts the child through the Trivium and is distinguished by the study of subjects such as Latin, logic and rhetoric.

Latin

Latin 1) provides an efficient way to learn the grammatical structure of English, 2) is the key to about fifty percent of English vocabulary, 3) is the key to all romance languages, 4) helps develop a precision of mind that is helpful in subjects such as science, and 5) appears frequently in Western literature. Latin should be studied first, as a springboard for Greek, since Greek is more difficult.

Latin can be taught from a book with no concern for pronunciation, because no culture today speaks Latin and no one is certain of the original pronunciation. Although there are classical and ecclesiastical pronunciations, the simplest method is to say it as though it were English. However, maintain consistency in pronunciation.

Logic

An *argument*, in logic, is a reason for believing something and an answer to the question, "Why?" It includes two parts—a group of one or more premises, and a conclusion. In logic, the student must first distinguish between the structure (skeleton, basic framework) of the argument and its content.

"Formal logic can be seen as part of mathematics and logical thought should be encouraged in all subjects."[4]

Rhetoric

Aristotle asserted that rhetoric is necessary in order to be persuasive. Classical (oral) rhetoric developed in the Greco-Roman world and revived during the Renaissance and Reformation. Rhetoric is divided into five canons. The first three are applicable to all communication, including essay and letter writing.

1) *Inventio*—arguments, illustrations and content are developed.
2) *Dispositio*—content is arranged in advantageous order.
3) *Elocutio*—one considers how best to say it all.
4) *Memoria*—speech is memorized.
5) *Pronuntiatio*—speech is delivered.

The Renaissance

The Renaissance encompassed discovery, exploration and inventions. A new appreciation of classical languages resulted in the revival of learning. Printing now made the study of classic works possible. Men suddenly found intensely human life in the tales of gods and goddesses. These myths became revelations of human expression, strength and beauty. The Renaissance men also noted that these works were written in a polished and charming style.

Petrarch (1304-1374)

Petrarch was the first great leader of the Renaissance. Boccacio, another leader, learned Greek and translated Homer, and also wrote *Decameron,* which inspired and provided material for the first great English poem, *Canterbury Tales,* by Chaucer. When Constantinople fell into the hands of the Turks in 1453, many Greek scholars fled to Italy carrying their literary treasures with them, expanding the resurgence of learning. Scholars in Italy focused on learning the classical languages so as to be able to read the classic literature of Greece and Rome.

Erasmus (1469-1536)

Erasmus was one of the greatest of all Renaissance humanists. He said that lessons should be adapted to the ability of the child and should be taught with sympathy and tenderness. He believed that all subjects should be subordinate to the classics. Geography and other subjects should be taught only for a greater understanding of the classics. He knew that politeness has a moral side, proceeding from the inner disposition of a well-ordered soul. Renaissance learning opened the way for a new intelligence and inspiration for many and struck a sturdy blow for human liberty.

The Primary School

The Primary School was the child of Protestantism and its cradle was the Reformation. Martin Luther believed that parents were responsible for their children's education before anyone else, but that the State had a duty to require regular attendance at school. However, Luther's school was not as structured as government schools are today. He said that children should attend school only one or two hours a day and then afterwards the boys should learn a trade at home, while the girls attend to home duties.

John Milton (1608-1674)

Best known for his Paradise Lost, Milton was already an accomplished scholar at the age of fifteen. Milton felt that being taught to appear to know was a root of all falsehood in life, society and professions. Today we have the deception of "teaching to the test" by teachers, and cramming for tests by students, wherein knowledge departs when the test is completed. Milton thought education should produce well-informed, moral citizens and that the parents' good example readily motivates the young child with a desire for doing right, as children want to be just like their parents.

Milton's Ideas

- Point out and name objects as Baby is taught to speak—the knowledge of words is best obtained by the early knowledge of things.
- Begin educating with interesting books that invite study and provoke thought. Language (literature) records the experience and traditions of other people and times and is how we acquire all information.
- Along with delightful books, provide careful instruction and explanation in order to stimulate love for learning. Teaching should arouse thought and exercise memory. If what is studied fails to become the property of the mind, learning is in vain.
- Review times tables and other facts.
- Go over the same subject matter in greater depth.
- Study math daily.
- Begin with easy topics, but learn thoroughly.
- Do not force ". . . the empty wits of children to compose themes and essays . . ." on subjects of which they know nothing.

Jean Jacques Rousseau (1712-1778)

Rousseau's theories influenced a long line of educators, beginning with Pestalozzi and continuing until this day. Napoleon considered Rousseau's *Social Contract* the cause of the French Revolution (World Book) and this work became its textbook. His educational treatise and romance, *Emile* (1762), was also controversial. His arrest was ordered, but he left the country. Emile is written in a clear, brilliant style, which may be the reason for its enduring influence. Its brightest feature is the love of nature pervading the book.

Johann Heinrich Pestalozzi (1746-1827)

Pestalozzi's father was a physician of great intelligence, but died before Johann was six years of age. His mother was a great influence on his life. Motivated by desire to relieve the burdened, Pestalozzi tried farming, ministry and law, before finding his calling as an educator. He gave up ministry because he felt inadequate in preaching; and law, because he realized that human law could never do away with injustice. His farming venture was also philanthropic—he wanted to teach peasants better methods. Pestalozzi believed education would free the oppressed. His first educational endeavor was a forerunner of our technical schools.

Pestalozzi's philosophy of education stemmed from his own experiences. He said, "The only sure foundation upon which we may hope to secure national culture and elevate the poor is that of the home where the love of the father and mother is the ruling principle." Pestalozzi was influenced by Rousseau and wanted to establish a "psychological method of instruction" that was in line with the laws of human nature. He placed a special emphasis on spontaneity and self-activity. He believed children should learn through the senses from real life—that they should be free to pursue their own interests and draw their own conclusions. They should not be given ready-made answers but should arrive at answers themselves. The child's seeing, judging and reasoning should be cultivated and self-activity encouraged.

Pestalozzi believed:

- Personality is sacred.
- In each child is the promise of his potentiality.
- Love of those we would educate is essential.
- Children should be taught with other children.
- All knowledge is obtained through the senses by the self-activity of the child.
- Objects should be used freely, especially with young children.
- The mother is the natural educator of the child in the early years and she should be educated herself. "Maternal love is the first agent in education . . . ."
- He used the phonics method, math manipulatives, relative grading (according to capacity of child), and taught all subjects through doing.

Although Pestalozzi disdained exact method, in his book, *How Gertrude Teaches her Children,* he attempts to explain his system and also how to apply the ideas of Comenius and Rousseau. The Home and Colonial School Society was the first school in England devoted to advancing the methods of Pestalozzi. In 1860, Charlotte Mason began her three-year training course there.

Charlotte Mason Homeschooling

Charlotte Mason was a British educator who lived and worked at the turn of the century. Her ideas had a great impact during her time and continue to influence an increasing number of educators today. Miss Mason believed that children should have a generous curriculum—characterized by nobility and forbearance, marked by abundance—with rich bouquet and flavor—the best of the best, and without limit. Miss Mason's books are also "generous," both in ideas and in words.

Although rich in ideas, I feel her thoughts could have been communicated in fewer words.

✗ Do as I did when reading her books, and use a highlighter to mine the many nuggets of gold.

Much of the following is directly quoted from Miss Mason's *A Philosophy of Education*⁵ and from back issues of *Parent's Review.* ☞ **The Charlotte Mason Research and Supply Company.**

Narration

Miss Mason said that children will be attentive to reading if interesting literary books are used, and if they know for certain that no second or third reading will be allowed. After the reading the child is to tell back the passage read, giving as much detail as he remembers. This is called narration.

> *Children must do the work for themselves. They must read the given pages and tell what they have read. . . . All school work should be conducted in such a manner that the children are aware of the responsibility of learning; it is their business to know that which has been taught. To this end the subject matter should not be repeated. . . . To allow repetition of a lesson is to shift the responsibility for it from the shoulders of the pupil to those of the teacher. . . . A single reading is a condition insisted upon because a naturally desultory [aimless] habit of mind leads us all to put off the effort of attention as long as a second or third chance of coping with the subject is to be hoped for.*

A Literary Feast

"The mind . . . has a natural preference for literary form. . . . oral teaching was to a great extent ruled out; a large number of books on many subjects were set for reading in morning school-hours; so much work was set that there was only time for a single reading; all reading was tested by a narration of the whole or a given passage, whether orally or in writing." Questions were to be asked only after the student's narration. Very little grammar teaching was needed.

Once children are allowed a due share in their own education . . . our chief concern for the mind or for the body is to supply a well-ordered table with abundant, appetizing, nourishing and very varied food, which children deal with in their own way and for themselves. This food must be served "au naturel," without the predigestion which deprives it of stimulating and nourishing properties, and no sort of forcible feeding or spoon feeding may be practiced. Hungry minds sit down to such a diet with the charming greediness of little children; they absorb it, assimilate it and grow thereby in a manner astonishing to those accustomed to the dull profitless ruminating [turning a matter over and over] . . . so often practiced in schools. . . . No rewards or punishments are necessary . . . students voluntarily, immediately, and perfectly give full attention to these lovely books. . . . Complete and entire attention is a natural function which requires no effort and causes no fatigue.

The teachers underrate the tastes and abilities of their pupils. . . . What they want is knowledge conveyed in literary form . . . give a child a few fit and exact words on the subject and he has the picture in his mind's eye, nay, a series, miles long of really glorious films; for a child's amazing vivifying imagination is part and parcel of his intellect.

The best available book is chosen and is read through perhaps in the course of two or three years. . . . No stray lessons are given on interesting subjects; the knowledge the children get is consecutive. . . . they know and write on any part of it [the day's reading] with ease and fluency, in vigorous English; they usually spell well. There are no revisions.

Miss Mason believed that the home should be a rich library. This library can be built, over time, without great expense: "Books . . . may be picked up at second-hand stalls with the obliterated names of half-a-dozen successive owners."

Among her suggestions for young children are *Andersen's Fairy Tales, Aesop's Fables, Pilgrim's Progress,* and *Just So Stories* by Kipling; later *Rob Roy* by Scott, Goldsmith's poems, Stevenson's *Kidnapped,* Shakespeare amd Homer.

History

I believe that Miss Mason would approve of autobiographies of famous people who lived and took part in history, such as those written by Benjamin Franklin, George Washington and Winston Churchill. She cautioned:

> *Not stories from history, but consecutive reading, say forty pages in a term, from a well-written, well-considered large volume which is also well-illustrated . . . [not pictures, but examples, incidents and anecdotes]. The work . . . is always chronologically progressive. . . . It is never too late to mend but may we not delay to offer such a liberal and generous diet of history to every child . . . as shall give weight to his decisions, consideration to his actions and stability to his conduct; that stability, the lack of which has plunged us into many a stormy sea of unrest.*

Math and Art

"Mathematics are to be studied for their own sake and not as they make for general intelligence and grasp of mind." Works of the masters are studied, one artist at a time, six paintings per term. Great paintings should not be copied lest the child loses reverence for the original, but they should "illustrate favorite scenes and passages in the books read during the term." This, along with narration, shows just how much the child is comprehending from the passages read.

Books dealing with science . . . should be of a literary character . . . and we should probably be more scientific as a people if we scrapped all the text-books which swell publisher's lists. . . . The principles which underlie science are at the same time so simple, so profound and so far-reaching that . . . these principles are therefore meet subjects for literary treatment, while the details of their application are so technical and so minute as—except by way of illustration—to be unnecessary for school work or for general knowledge.

However, Miss Mason believed there was a place for field and laboratory work and encouraged nature study with notebooks in which the child sketched and wrote descriptions of what they were observing.

Samuel Wilderspin (1792-1866)

Do you think today's preschools for three- to five-year-old children are a new thing? Infant Schools actually began in the early 1800s and were similar to today's early preschools or daycare centers. Wilderspin thought that the schools were needed to give more supervision than the busy mother could provide at home. Children were taught what was useful and helpful but their primary aim was to form within the child good habits and a cheerful disposition. Wilderspin's leading idea was to adapt the teaching to the nature of the child. The children remained in the school for two or three years, after which they were admitted to a more advanced school, where they were taught to read, write and do arithmetic. Later, Wilderspin's schools deteriorated into either places of amusement or—the complete opposite—schools where dry, hard, scientific words took the place of ideas and the physical world.

Johann Friedrich Herbart (1776-1841)

Herbart's mother was a great influence on his education. She even studied Greek with him. She was gentle and yet firm in discipline. Eventually Herbart's parents separated. After University and a short time as a tutor, he went for further study. Herbart knew Pestalozzi and was impressed with him. It is said that Herbart elevated education to a science. It seems to me that he was instrumental in complicating a simple process. Yet, he had a worthy goal of well-rounded men.

Friedrich Froebel (1782-1852)

Friedrich Froebel is considered the father of the kindergarten. Like Pestalozzi, whose work influenced him greatly, Froebel's education was neglected in his early years. Although he began his four years of school at age ten, it does not appear that he made much progress. Like Pestalozzi, Froebel attempted various short-lived enterprises until finding his niche in education. Froebel's philosophy is found in *Education of Man*.

Horace Mann (1796-1859)

Horace Mann believed that a free, intelligent and moral people could only be realized by public education. Mann nearly single-handedly enabled nation-wide public education. He did a colossal work in drawing together funding and administration. Although he prophetically said there should be ". . . a free, straight, solid pathway by which [the child] can walk directly up from the ignorance of an infant to a knowledge of the primary duties of man," he could not have imagined the scope of today's public education from kindergarten through high school. He established free schools, founded normal schools to train teachers, encouraged milder forms of discipline, and improved schoolhouses.

John Dewey (1859-1952)

Some of John Dewey's beliefs:

- Students are to be trained to be productive members of the group.
- Students are to be stimulated to act for the good of the group.
- Educational activity—what the child learns and how much he accomplishes—must arise from the child's desires, not from external structure or preset subject matter.
- Education is to be project-oriented.
- The child's individual tendencies are to be directed toward co-operative living.

•❖ You may now wish to go back and amend your own *philosophy of education*. Add any new or amplified thoughts to your notebook. To do your own study of the history of education, see ☞ **Endnotes** or search for information on the educator of your choice at:

www.google.com

Other Homeschooling Methods

Unschooling

Unschooling is *the* hands-off method. Learning is totally or primarily child-directed. Your child can study whatever topics he is interested in. Because of this, he will apply himself more diligently to learning. When state regulations specify that we must spend a certain number of hours at schooling, many of us feel compelled to spend all of this time in a very structured setting—no matter if we are destroying our relationship with our children and their desire to learn in the process! Unschooling would alleviate this pressure. Learning materials should be available in abundance—such as those from the library. If you can purchase items related to your child's interests, so much the better but this is not always necessary, if free or on-hand resources are used.

For more information see ☞ *F.U.N. News* and ☞ *Home Education Magazine.*

Relaxed

Author and speaker, Mary Hood, Ph.D. says:

> *I definitely differentiate the "relaxed" method of homeschooling from unschooling because of my emphasis on underlying structure, including . . . underlying time frame for the day, emphasis on long range goals and the role of the parent which definitely includes filling in perceived gaps along the way to those goals.*[6]

Mary tells how to get started if your child has recently been taken out of a school. The parent can tell the child that each day he must do something related to learning.

> *If the kids have no idea what you are talking about, you can give them suggestions: "You could read a book or write a story or a letter to Grandma, or do some work in your math book." I would also have a regular story time where I read interesting books to them. . . . By helping a child develop more responsibility for his own learning, you can help him develop self-discipline.*[7]

✔ Mary Hood says to assign classics when children are reading too many lower quality books. Written and oral communication skill is the primary prerequisite for college. She also recommends having students do term papers for college preparation.

The Moore Formula

Dr. Raymond and Dorothy Moore grandparented this method of study. The Moore Formula combines school with work and service, and garnishes it with a healthful, wise lifestyle. This philosophy says that the most important qualifications for parents are warm responsiveness and a "fairly decent basic education."[8]

This method is similar to unschooling in some ways—the parent does not provide workbooks, but plenty of time for the child to pursue his interests. However, it is not recommended that all assignments and formal work be eliminated altogether.

The Moore formula recommends no formal schooling until the child is eight or twelve, especially if a boy, because all learning necessary to prepare for high school can be accomplished in only two or three years. This delay and concentration will result in a more successful student. Even though it is suggested that the parent wait to start formal schooling, the parent should not neglect to read to, and respond to, their children from their earliest age.

"Delay + Concentration = Success"

✔ Determine when you will begin serious study and do concentrated, very disciplined tutoring during this two- to three-year period. You must first determine exactly what comprises a good education, and make your plan for those years. Previous to this period, let your child's life be filled with play, lots of read-alouds, independent reading, work, journaling, family business and perhaps a few scholastic endeavors (but not filled with video, computer games or TV!). Let him know early that when he reaches the designated age, formal schooling will begin. Should you use a curriculum's placement testing previous to formal schooling, you may find that much progress has been made without even trying, because of your informal literary foundation.

Moore Philosophy

The Moore philosophy says that spending more time with peers (than parents) before age eleven or twelve causes peer dependency. Children who feel needed, wanted and depended upon have the best self-confidence. The longer they are taught at home, the higher this self-concept. Homeschooled students *do* develop the ability to think things through maturely and consistently from five to eight years earlier than conventionally schooled children.

Sensible and easy, proven to give great results, the Moore formula as described in ☞ ***The Successful Homeschool Family Handbook*** provides meat for every homeschooler to "chew on" and "digest." This book provides a six-page summary of the Formula. The book not only arrests and stimulates, but also—more importantly— motivates to action. The bottom line: Be a loving, responsive parent and respect your kids.

Moore Methods

✔ Rely on discussion and project learning, but don't neglect drill for mastery of basics. Ask "why?" and "how?" more than what, when, where and how much. Have fun with your children. Be a good example and warmly share companionship with your children throughout the day. Be extremely selective in choosing materials or workshops. Make sure materials are easy to use.

Family industry and service are not electives. Teach service—first at home, then elsewhere. Share family management and family business. "Students who work with their hands develop common sense and practical skills, and do much better with their heads."[9]

The Robinson Curriculum

The Robinson Curriculum consists of an easy schedule— math first, a one-page essay, and then reading for a number of hours. The CD set we used included the complete set of the 1911 *Encyclopedia Britannica,* the 1913 *Webster's Dictionary,* plus nearly three hundred other scholarly and children's books. It also included vocabulary lists, exams and essay questions. Zephi eventually completed her schooling at home at age sixteen, entirely on her own, by completing the RC booklist and doing advanced Saxon courses. See more about Zephi and her graduation speech in ❀ *Easy Homeschooling Companion.*

Dr. Robinson—a scientist—says that there is no need to dissect a frog to learn the circulatory system. I like this approach to science, and the method's literary focus in all subjects. The use of primary sources (writings by those who lived the history) make the course valuable. I also like the independent study techniques. You may get more information about this method and other options for doing lower-cost, Robinson-*style* educating from ☞ **Home School Treasures.**

12
Building a Business

You have unique talents! As your children grow, your confidence and skills will also grow. You may find yourself thinking of a home business and with the children home, there is the possibility of a family business. Your young adults may need guidance for their future life-choices. "The Right Business," below, is especially appropriate for them.

Ideally, mothering will be your full-time business when your children are small. Perhaps your business idea is for a later time in your life—when they are grown and living on their own. You do not want to look back with longing on the family that grew much too fast while you were taking care of business. However, if you are already working at a job or business, there are easy ways to combine that with homeschooling, which I will share later in the chapter.

Family Business

If you can put each of the children to work with you, a business idea is a good thing that will contribute greatly to your children's education. The children must be involved in the business on a daily basis. Have specific jobs planned for them to do with you. They must work at it as often or nearly as often as the parents do. See more about the value of family business in Dr. Raymond Moore's books.

When I think about family business, I think about a small grocery or retail store or an income-producing farm. There are farms in our area where the children do not take part in the work, because of public school activities, or the general laziness of today's children—perhaps both. It was not like this a few decades ago. These agri-businessmen called on *our sons* to help, knowing that they are hard workers and available. Many homeschoolers have opened curriculum businesses, with the children doing packing, shipping and toting to curriculum fairs. Selling a tangible product—as opposed to writing or other individual creative work—would be a better family business. With a product, there are always simple tasks to do such as packaging, organizing, labeling, hauling and sometimes—depending on the child's age—selling.

It takes money to make money!

Businesses often—and often for a long time—cost more than they make. Instead of adding to the family's budget, you may drain it even more by starting a business. Break-even point is when business expenses are are finally met by business income. Because of this startup period, many businesses don't make it. You must be prepared. Do not make the mistake of going into business when you have immediate needs or limited funds. Do not attempt to "open your doors" until you have more than the most money that you think you will need to take care of your business "baby" as well as the other babies in your family for a number of years. Home businesses are the least expensive to start, but there are always some expenses. The largest expenses for home businesses are equipment, expansion, advertising and—if you sell a product—inventory. It is better not to start at all than to have to quit after spending many years and many dollars promoting a business.

Business Readiness

During your time of preparation—which could be months, or even years—your tasks are to:
1) Save specifically for your business.
2) Decide what kind of business to start.
3) Research business, generally and specifically.

While you are putting away money for business start-up costs, you can be "homeschooling" yourself. Your library has an abundance of business books, magazines and videos—possibly even some about the particular business that you are considering. Some libraries also have scanners, printers and other equipment. I actually started our business at the library using their computers and printers.

Take advantage of every business learning opportunity that you can. If you can afford to go to conferences, do so. Buy books if you can. Check out business videos or buy them. Do all the learning you can before "opening your doors"—you may not have time for it after! See "Resources" for suggested ☞ **Business Books.**

The Right Business

Here is another notebook idea to pinpoint exactly what kind of business would be best for you, or business or career for your young adult. It is ideal if you have a large chunk of time available; however, you may take a break and return to this project later. When returning, you will probably have thought of other things you can add.

➥ Gather several pages of notebook paper and a good pen. You are going to list everything you have ever done—not just the jobs you have had, but every single thing that you can remember doing. For example: sawing wood, watching TV, going down the river on a raft, playing a game. It might help to think about different "hats" you have worn and then list what was done done in that capacity. To keep your papers more orderly, use headings, such as "Homeschool Teacher." Then list activities done under that heading. As you start writing, your thoughts will start flowing and more and more things will pop into your mind. Just a few words for each listing is sufficient, but make sure you put down everything that you can think of. Ask a close friend or family member if they can help with these recollections. I filled seventeen pages! Although time-consuming, this is foundational for picking the perfect business or career.

Now look over your list and circle all of those things that you really enjoyed doing. Then next to each circled listing, put an "A" for those things you do well, a "B" for those things you do not do well and a "C" for those things that you do not do well, but would like to improve—and can improve—such as typing speed.

You may wish to list separately all the items that you circled, especially the "A's" and the "C's." Study your lists. The fun begins! You will see a pattern emerging. You will discover that you have enjoyed similar tasks and disliked similar tasks. As a result of this brainstorming session, you will probably see a business or career emerging that will tie together all of your skills and talents and desires and be the best choice for you.

In *Write It Down, Make It Happen,* Henriette Anne Klauser says to write things as if they had already happened. While this doesn't apply to the above project it does apply to your dreams and goals in this area of business. She says that fiction becomes non-fiction, giving several examples in her book of that happening.

Other Preparation

"Find a need and fill it." Good advice. Find out if there is a market for what you plan to do. You can post questions related to your product or business service on appropriate forums, blogs or chats. I have written articles based on input gathered in this manner.

Write a business plan. Although most often used for the purpose of getting business financing, a business plan can be a map that will help you get to where you want to go in business. To learn basic accounting systems get *Small Time Operator*. Look for this book at your public library.

After you have accumulated startup costs and a store of knowledge, and after carefully considered your decision, plunge in! A family friend, who had been involved in many businesses, gave me some simple and yet profound advice. He said, "Just do it!" One can talk and talk, prepare and dream but sometimes this is the best advice. If you start wisely—in your home, without debt and with savings—there is little financial risk involved, therefore little to be apprehensive about.

As your business awaits a burst of success, do not get discouraged if there are days, weeks, or even months when the money does not come in. So just keep at it, when you are not busy with your family. Do a little every day and success will come!

Whew! You made it through the startup period. You have become wildly successful! But now you will be wildly busy as well, which will take you away from your family even more. Or you will be forced to to grow and expand—hire others or move, or both—which will eliminate the hominess of a home business and take you even farther away from the home circle. However, if you are already a "sole" proprietor, you can explore new options and tasks to draw your children into the business with you.

Write detailed job descriptions for each child.

Marketing

Marketing includes advertising, but much more than advertising. When a homeschool book seller gives a talk at a convention or a local support group, she is marketing. When two companies swap flyers to use for inserts in the packages they send out—they are marketing. When you write a personal letter to a customer or potential customer, you are marketing. Marketing can be loosely defined as anything that is done that could result in sales. There are free marketing activities.

If you have a unique product or idea, and can write reasonably well, you can market by writing articles. Most publications would rather let you add a tag line about your business than pay you. And those few lines may be more profitable than being paid for the article, especially if the publication has a large circulation.

You can buy an inexpensive brochure holder and ask related businesses to display your brochure. (Be sure to check back regularly to refill.) Place posters on bulletin boards everywhere, and check back regularly and re-post if necessary.

Think bartering. Always offer something besides cash in return for what you want. You may be surprised at how many businesses are willing to do this. Offer to speak to groups whose members might be interested in your expertise. Many times you can sell at this time. If not, pass out simple information sheets with contact information. My favorite book on general marketing is ☞ *Guerrilla Marketing* by Jay Levinson. It includes many low-cost ideas. Look for books on marketing for your specific field. I have several on book marketing, each packed with more ideas than I find time to use.

You may choose to do Internet marketing. This alone can be quite effective. There are various bulletin boards where you may post free ads for your product or service.

Again, search out books and websites on marketing and productivity. Business topics have filled many books and I could never do them justice in one small chapter. One of my favorite no-nonsense writers and productivity coaches is Brian Tracy.

Networking

Business networking is connecting and interacting with others with the motive that they become future customers, or a future help to one's business. Networking was one thing I skipped over in the business books I read. The concept seemed so self-serving! What homeschooling mom would have the time to form the relationships and join the clubs, anyhow? I found that networking can be natural, leading to close friendships, along with free advertising, free publicity, endorsements from well-known people, free subscriptions, bartered subscriptions and five times the going rate for articles!

My products may be similar to the others in my network, but we are not competitors. We have each been in business approximately the same time. We are learning together and yet we have our own special niche.

Advertising

Advertising can be very expensive, and often it seems those dollars are tossed into the wind. Your product must be a mid- to high-cost item to merit expensive advertising in a consumer magazine. These ads are best left to established businesses whose products do sell, and who have a high income with an established customer base.

✗ Contact the publications that you consider best for your particular product and ask for their advertising rate sheets. Ask these questions first about each publication: What is the circulation? (How many readers are there?) Ask yourself, "Are these readers people who would be interested in my product?" Then:

1) Pick the absolute best *one* publication for your product.
2) Decide on a small display ad or a classified ad.
3) Study other ads and write yours based on what response you want. One of our best ads was a longer classified written in narrative. I believe it attracted people because it sounded more personal.
4) Include in your start-up costs enough funds to cover three to twelve months of insertions in this one publication.
5) Start with one insertion. If proceeds from this ad cover the cost, make a longer, three- to six-month commitment with the same publication.

If you made money off your ad, don't make the mistake of spending it before re-advertising, or sales may trickle to a stop. Regarding business expenditures, advertising should be first. Keep it simple. If a publication's ads are making money, stay with it. Don't make the mistake of scattering your money to the four winds—to a multitude of different publications. Later when you are ready to expand, you can add one publication at a time.

Homeschooling While Working

Even if you work outside the home, you can homeschool. If you are working at a job or business twenty hours a week, another twenty at homeschooling would be only equivalent to a full time job. Even with working forty hours a week at a job or business, you can still teach your children at home. If you read a few hours each night, your child's skills would surpass those of public-school students, whose parents have to spend the evenings reteaching the things the children haven't learned at school.

Those of you who have a seasonal business or just work certain months of the year may schedule school for the months that your business is slower, or for the months that you are not working. A twelve-month schedule would be ideal for some. Spend about three hours each evening, and four or five on Saturday at schooling. You may spend even less time at school, depending on 1) your state's requirements, 2) whether your child can do independent study, and 3) how much informal learning you plan to do.

The weekend would be ideal for hands-on learning along with workbooks, reading and field trips. Workbooks and flash cards work well for math. You may wish to supplement your science reading with experiments. There are many books available on experiments that can be done with simple materials.

See "Starting Up," Chapter 2, for details on what and how to teach. Be sure to use subject combining (Chapter 6) to save time. This is one of the most important techniques for busy working moms.

Child Care

You and your husband might be able to stagger your working hours. He works while you are home; you work while he teaches and cares for the children; or vica versa. If you are using the schools as a care giver, here are some suggestions:

1) Time share care with a friend—while one of you works, the other teaches one or two subjects to the children. While you are working, your older children could be either doing some of their schoolwork, or helping your friend with the younger children.
2) Your older child could be working, possibly as an apprentice in a chosen field.
3) Your older child could be babysitting and teaching your younger children.
4) Your older child could be doing school work and keeping up the house.
5) Your younger children could be at a day care center or relative's house. Your children are being taught life skills as well as academics so they will be a blessing, not a burden, to others.

Is your child enrolled in a private school? Homeschooling could save you money. With *Easy Homeschooling* you can provide a high quality education for much less. With so many money-saving helps and ideas, you may find that you can live without an extra income and become a full-time homeschooling mom.

Tips from Working Mothers

Simplify your schedule. Downscale. If you go shopping twice a week, start going once. If once a week, go once every two weeks. Stay home. Organize. Be judicious about cutting the fat out—in every area of your life: Curriculum. Possessions. Activities. Try alternating days for business and school.

Shari Henry
Author of *Homeschooling: The Middle Years*
Allow children complete access, including them in all chores, meal prep . . . filling their tanks emotionally. Then, insist on a time of quiet for each person and get busy. . . .

Deb Deffinbaugh
The Timberdoodle Company

So how do we do it all in schoolwork? By insisting on a system of accountability for each child. We have found that children will accomplish far more and learn far better when we stop hovering over them. Children sincerely desire to have as much control as possible over their lives, and this is a wonderful way to introduce them to the adult world of responsibilities and consequences.

Anne Olwin
Artist and art teacher

Prepare ahead of time for deadlines. Have snacks and other activities on hand for young ones. Involve the children—sure it's easier to do it yourself, but you're missing an opportunity for training them in life skills if you fail to involve them. It saves time in the long run. Laugh! Keep a good sense of humor—everything is more difficult and takes longer if you don't.

Five years later, Anne adds: The importance of faithfulness in raising and homeschooling my children cannot be overstated. In that season my home business was small, but I learned to make the most of my time and I honed my skills. Now that the children are grown, I reap the rewards of a close strong family . . . and the art business is exploding in a way I could not have envisioned then.

Leese Griffith
Writer, small business owner

I try to combine errands whenever possible, and "work" mainly during afternoon quiet time and after the boys go to bed. When a big job comes in and I am juggling too much, we slack off a bit during the day and Daddy does more in the evenings—like listening to our oldest read, or doing projects.

Catherine White

Former editor of *An Encouraging Word*

Fit school in—don't be rigid. Sometimes fit work in. Simplify housework and cooking, extracurricular activities, life—eliminate TV, stay home and run errands on one day. Don't collect knickknacks that clutter your home and life by having to take care of them.

Shelli Owen

Formerly of The Homeschool Supply House

I. Overlap tasks.
- Bedtime stories and literature
- Counting games, identifying colors, shapes and letter sounds, while walking or driving

II. Simplify life
- Fewer things to take care of—smaller house, fewer store-bought toys for kids
- Organization
- Sharing of house and yard work (chores)

If I do these things, then everything else seems to fall into place—if not immediately, eventually.

Nancy Greer

☞ **F.U.N. News and Books**

Include your children in your work if you can. They will learn lots of important skills that many adults don't have. Our children have learned that if the business phone rings, they need to do a quiet activity. . . . Let your child do as much as is safe. Our son can prepare his own breakfast and lunch if needed. He's proud of it, and he's learning important skills. Also—you're going to have to decide what's important. If you work, something else is going to have to give. Maybe the laundry piles up some, or you don't dust as often. You may be able to do everything for a while, but your sanity or health will suffer eventually.

Beth Nieman
Librarian, Carlsbad, NM

On days when I work, I cook supper right after breakfast! I work evenings, so I'm not home for supper. My family likes casseroles, chilis, lasagna, stews and similar items. I bake the main course in the morning and start a loaf of bread in my bread machine, timing it so that the bread will be done when my family is ready for supper. Sometimes I prepare salad or dessert as well. I put a portion of whatever I've made aside to take with me for my dinner break, and put the rest in the refrigerator for my family to heat and eat. I still get to enjoy cooking, we save money by eating out less, my family gets a hot meal every night, and there's no pressure on my husband to fix dinner when he is tired after work.

Martha Greene
www.MarmeeDear.com

"We school on a year-round schedule," says Martha Greene, homeschooling mother to eleven, author, and owner of Marmee's Kitchen, "This leaves most weeks for school days as four-day weeks, keeping Fridays and Saturdays free for the business. I try to make it a policy to either get up very early and take care of business emails or only work on the business when all the school work is done."

Martha Greene's advice is from ☞ **HomeGrown Business,** *an ebook in which home-school graduates and business owners, Jesse and Crystal Paine, share stories of twenty-nine families who successfully own and operate a business while homeschooling.*

Angie Blackman

Editor-in-Chief, *Homeschooling Horizons Magazine*

www.homeschoolinghorizons.com

With my flexible work hours, I do schoolwork with the kids in the morning, errands and activities in the afternoon and work in the evening after the kids are in bed. It also helps that my husband works evenings—so that I'm not ignoring him! My sanity-savers are my crockpot (slow cooker) and + Once-A-Month Cooking.

Crockpot days are easy—I simply drop a roast, veggies, spices and about half a cup of water in and set it for eight to ten hours. Supper is ready by 6:00 P.M. *Ultra easy.* To make it even easier, after unpacking the groceries, rather than throwing the meats and such into the freezer, I first drop them into a ziplock bag with a marinade. The ingredients will season while frozen. The night before I want to serve this dish, I'll defrost the roast in the fridge so that in the morning I am simply slipping it out of the marinade and into the crockpot. *Wonderfully easy.*

"Once a Month" cooking, though, is my biggest time saver. It sounds like it would be a major undertaking to cook up thirty to forty meals in one weekend, but is it ever awesome to know that I can run to the freezer on a busy night and throw a precooked frozen meal into the microwave to defrost and reheat! All in under forty minutes, and those thirty to forty meals last a whole lot longer than one month! On average, we'll make them last about six weeks, having spaghetti, a crockpot or a pizza night balancing out the week. The meals also provide a lot of variety. Six to eight different meals are made in quantity so that each meal can be had on five different days.

The key to working and homeschooling is having a routine and finding a balance. If you know that you have work hours on a certain day, balance those hours with at home-family hours. Because of my flexible schedule, I work primarily a four- to six-hour "day" in the evenings. 2:00 A.M. is my bedtime on those days. Homeschooling's flexibility allows me to sleep in until 8:00 A.M., so it's not like I am not getting enough sleep at night—I just keep a Pacific time schedule while living on the

East Coast! If you adjust your work around family and home, life flows nicely. When work starts taking over your time, you know that someone will be losing out—your family and you. Find that balance and you will have both prosperity and a happy home.

13

Sailing through High School

For EasyHomeschoolers, high school is a smooth transition with more of the same and only minor differences. There will be more and greater literature, more extra-curricular activities, more service, and more emphasis on excellence. High school is also the time for deeper individual studies and for exploring careers and colleges. The previous chapter, "Building a Business," detailed a notebook plan to help your young adults discover what calling they are best suited for.

By this time your child should have ⊸ listed his dreams, goals and the steps needed to meet those goals. (See instructions throughout this book.) Some of these goals may have been met by now. With goals in place, learning will also fall into place as the step lists are worked in the direction of your young adult's goals.

> *It is crucial that the students themselves make these plans, rather than their parents. Unless the teens have had significant input into the planning phase, they will generally be recalcitrant when it comes to putting forth the required effort.*[1]

Antique and Classic Books

College is a means to an end and not the end in itself. Your child should have goals beyond college. If college is a step to those goals, they should begin preparation while in high school.

A priority for high school is that you guide your child into more depth in literature. Great literature produces great minds. For high school, use more of the same, and even greater selections.

Now your student may read Shakespeare, *The Federalist Papers,* Machiavelli, Dumas and the Greek classics. For fifteen- to eighteen-year-olds, Charlotte Mason suggested Pope's *Essay on Man,* Carlyle's *Essay on Burns,* Goldsmith's *Citizen of the World,* Thackeray's *The Virginians, The Oxford Book of Verse* and Plutarch. Miss Mason also said that for this age, ". . . some definite teaching in the art of composition is advisable, but not too much, lest the young scholars be saddled with a stilted style which may encumber them for life."[2] Round out your young adult's studies with the lighter classic authors such as Steinbeck, Austen, Stevenson, Scott and Alcott—if they haven't been read yet. See Easy Homeschooling Companion, "Loving Literature," for learning techniques and more recommended books and authors.

Reading Aloud

Don't think that your students are now too old for read-aloud times. However, now you may wish to direct them into deeper research and skills such as—with poetry, for instance—actually practicing writing poems and dramatization. Your students are now also able to think more deeply about a subject and discuss it more thoroughly. Present questions that require reflection. Some questions may not even have an answer. However, these questions stimulate the thought process, which is what we want to cultivate in our children.

Cultivate your student's thought process!

Independent Study

Your students can do independent study from antique books. It helps to have a system of accountability. Do not neglect to enforce completion of assignments. Expect papers—summaries of what they have read. Do not let your students go one day with an overdue assignment. If they are allowed to miss

deadlines and not finish projects, they will not learn the valuable traits of completing what they have begun. Term papers and reports can be done using antique books for reference. Most have a wealth of interesting facts and ideas.

With a bedrock of the solid content of antique books, your children will graduate with sound, thoughtful minds.

Science & Math

Continue with a good math program such as *Saxon*. Our girls began Algebra in seventh grade and used the *Saxon* texts throughout high school. *Key to Algebra* should be used before *Saxon* Algebra to facilitate comprehension of algebraic concepts. Our younger daughter, Zephi, did *Key to Algebra* before Algebra 1, and was whizzing through the *Saxon* books with no problems whatsoever, whereas Jessica—who hadn't done *Key to Algebra* first, had problems. But *Key to Algebra* cannot stand alone. After completing the workbooks, Zephi could not complete the *Saxon Algebra 1* test. (*Key to Algebra* is a workbook series, widely available from homeschool catalogs.)

For science, your high schooler can study scientists and their discoveries. Investigate and duplicate the scientific experiments of noteworthy scientists for lab work. Require reports about these lab experiments. Have them dig deeper and thoroughly investigate each theory, including their opinions and thoughts.

Keeping Credits

Although high school is a smooth and often unnoticeable transition from the early grades, there is a difference. Colleges expect transcripts (a record of the high school classes and grades given for each). Therefore, in high school, any and all activities should be recorded. These will include cleaning, cooking, washing vehicles, teaching a little sister and writing a term paper. Even the most ordinary activity will be credited to "Life Skills" or "Home Economics."

You do not need to keep credits when you use a text—such as math—because completion of the book fulfills the required credit hours per year. But do keep track of time spent on activities related to that subject. Reading and reporting on a book titled *The History of Algebra,* for instance, may be needed for speech credits when computing is done in the senior year. Record everything in case you need to fill in gaps later. Don't forget art and Shakespeare videos, field trips and so on!

It works best to have the children keep the credits themselves, although you may need to remind them until it becomes habit. Check regularly to see that it is being done.

➥ Use a large three-ring binder with index dividers for each subject. Notebook paper "timesheets" for each subject will be placed before their reports or other school papers in that section of the notebook. You may have several timesheets for each subject. Start with one for each.

How to Calculate Credit Hours

- Make separate "timesheets" for each of the topics your high schooler covers (such as Global Studies) and place them in the proper section of the notebook. Choose the topic heading that will most likely fit the activity. At the top left of the notebook paper write the topic heading such as Global Studies, Home Economics, or Life Skills. Label it "Other," if you do not know where to put it. Later it may be easier to place these unusual activities where they need to go.
- On the top right, place a subheading such as "China," if the topic is Global Studies. (On the "Other" time-sheet you do not have to note a subheading.)
- Draw a narrow column on the right side of the paper.
- Draw two narrow columns on the left. Leave most of the space in the center for a description of the activity. If necessary, you may use several lines for each activity.
- On the right, record the actual hours spent on each individual activity or class, using decimals instead of fractions for portions of the hour, to make totaling the hours easier at year's end.

- In the center section of the page, tell what was done at that time.
- In one of the columns to the left, if applicable, place a reference number such as "GS-3" (Global Studies, Paper 3) which will also go on any paper or report related to that activity.
- In the second column on the left side of the paper, alongside the above reference number, insert a grade from that paper or report.
- At the end of each year, add up—or have your son or daughter add up—the actual hours spent at each subject.
- List the total hours on another "master chart" for that year. All subjects can be on one paper on this sheet. Along with listing hours actually spent per subject, you should average the grades given on reports or other projects for that subject, and record a final grade for each subject.
- Now you can find the credit hours earned for that year. In a classroom setting, much time is wasted as the teacher gives out instructions, hands out worksheets or makes other announcements. The schools use 120-180 hours for each credit. Since homeschooling is so efficient, we can use 140 hours or possibly even less to compute our credits. Divide the actual hours by 140 (140 actual hours = 1 credit hour). How many credit hours should you have? 20-32 is customary for graduation; 5-8 per year. To get an exact figure of credits needed for graduation in your state, check with a local high school or your state's department of education. If your child has a particular college in mind, you should check with them as well. Along with grades and credit hours, the transcript must have the student's date of birth and date of departure from school. You can find sample or blank transcripts on the Internet.
- Staple or clip the corresponding timesheets to the report papers that your student has written, subject by subject. Place the stack in a nine-by-thirteen manila envelope. If necessary use one envelope per subject. Label the outside of envelope with the subject (or topic if you have many, many papers), school year, and total hours for that subject. Then file all the envelopes away in a box or use a large rubber band to bind them together with a

copy of your master chart of total credits for that year. Keep in a safe place! Especially keep your "master chart" safe, and keep duplicate copies—perhaps in several formats—paper, computer and disk.

Credit keeping is a continual activity because each day is made up of many activities. When reviewing your child's annual credit hours you may find them short. Don't be concerned. You will balance things out in the next years of high school by focusing more on the areas where more credits are needed. Here are the credit hours required for high school graduation in one state. The credit hours required for the advanced course (college preparatory) follow the standard chart.

Standard High School Course

4.0 English
4.0 Social Studies (W. History, A. History, Gov., Economics)
4.0 Mathematics (Include Algebra I & Geometry)
4.0 Science (Include Biology I and any Physical Science)
1.0 Physical Education (or approved substitute)
0.5 Health Education
0.5 Computer Applications
5.5 Electives

Advanced Course

All of the above, plus:

2.0 Foreign Language (all the same language)
0.5 Fine Arts
Algebra II and Trigonometry (same total math hours).
Electives are reduced to 3.5

College

More and more colleges recruit the independent-thinking, well-prepared homeschool student. Jessica began sending for college catalogs at fourteen after reading, ☞ *Home School, High School and Beyond.*

Open Admissions Colleges

Open admissions colleges admit anyone over eighteen or with a high school diploma. Standardized college admissions testing is not required, nor is any particular high school course selection. Grades in high school are not relevant. Students who have not taken an academic preparatory program in high school may need to complete some high school level courses before taking college courses for credit toward a college degree. Such courses are usually available as remedial classes and may be taken at the college.

Rarely, if ever, is one asked for the actual diploma with the granting institution's seal. It is usually only a question on job applications. "Do you have a diploma or an equivalent?" The GED is the diploma option we have used for all of our children. We avoided having to have a transcript (for some) by having the child leave school before applying for the GED. With Zephi we had more red tape because she was under the preferred age. Contact your Adult Basic Education board to find the requirements for your state. Sometimes this group is affiliated with a city or community college. In Nebraska, the students are well-prepared for the test by GED classes. A no-cost ceremony and a reception are also provided in some communities.

Selective Admissions Colleges

Applicants to selective colleges must meet the criteria set by that particular college. Schools with selective criteria may look for students with high grade-point averages, rigorous academic preparation, high scores on the standardized college admissions tests, strong personal qualities and evidence of achievement. Some colleges are more selective than others. Selective colleges may require applicants to submit high school grade-point averages and rank in class, scores on standardized admissions tests (SAT or ACT) and letters of recommendation. Some may require a personal interview, and some may be particularly interested in the student's extracurricular activities. Get SAT prep books and software from your public library.

Life Skills

Perhaps more important than knowledge or a college education, are the skills that your adult children will use almost every day. These can be learned throughout your child's homeschooling years, but should be mastered in high school, if not previously. Young adults can learn sewing, cooking, finances, hair-cutting, auto upkeep, household repair and so on.

Our first skills class was "Quilting." I began by assigning a small antique book which included the history of quilting. Next the girls looked through quilting books and designed patterns. Their grandmother gave us many quilts, afghans and appliqued quilt tops, so the girls were given the option to use one of her quilt tops or start from scratch.

Another life skills unit could be "Cooking." Your child would plan menus for a week, shop, cook all the meals for a week—including the side dishes and breads, create a recipe, write a paper on cooking techniques, and help with bulk cooking for the freezer. ☞ ***Dinner's in the Freezer!*** is a guidebook for this big family project.

Life Skill Class
1) Research the subject.
2) Report, including what knowledge or steps are needed to become skilled in that area.
3) Learn the skill through hands-on training and experience. Let this be acquired over a long period of time. A week or two will not train for life. Better to have your young adult take over your finances or car care for the year, or until leaving home.

A World of Options
By Janice Campbell
www.EverydayEducation.com

When you make the decision to homeschool through the teen years, you open the door to many exciting options for your student. Teens not only have the opportunity to develop as individuals, but they can also pursue special interests, start microbusinesses, travel, accelerate their education, sample different careers, and more. Let's look at each option.

Special Interests. Have you noticed who is winning spelling and geography bees, music competitions and chess tournaments, debates and robotics competitions? Homeschooled students are often at the very top of these competitions. Why? It's because they have time to pursue special interests. If they want to spend three hours a day practicing violin, there are no deadlines. They don't have to put down the violin after 45 minutes and go rushing off to Algebra or soccer. A homeschooler's world is a world almost without deadlines, which means that time can be spent for things that really matter.

Microbusiness. What could be better than a summer job flipping burgers? Entrepreneurship, for one thing. Just think—instead of spending time in a mindless entry-level job, teens can start and run small businesses, and not only earn money for the future, but also learn about planning, budgeting, organization, marketing, and customer service, and perhaps even gain experience for a future career.

What kind of businesses can be operated as a microbusiness (small scale, no loans, minimal overhead)? Service-based businesses include tutoring, web design, pet sitting, calligraphy, landscape maintenance, and many others. Product-based businesses include selling produce, flowers, or baked goods, jewelry making, leather- or wood-crafting, or selling items on eBay. Almost any business that can be headquartered from home has potential to be a microbusiness.

Travel. There are few things more educational than travel. Homeschooled teens have the flexibility to travel at any time during the year, and if they happen to have a microbusiness and need to travel for it, they may even be able to deduct some of their travel expenses from their taxes! Family vacations tend to be less expensive and more pleasant when taken during off-peak seasons—homeschoolers don't need to wait for summer break! I took our boys on a two-month trip around the country one year—it was a geography, history, and culture lesson rolled into a very memorable package. We've also taken a wonderful 2-1/2 week trip to Europe, and several shorter trips in the States, all on a very tight budget. Homeschooling offers families the opportunity to travel for competitions, for business, and for pleasure whenever and wherever they want to go.

Accelerated Education. Why spend four years just doing high school, when you could exert a little more effort and earn college credit at the same time? By taking full advantage of college-level exams, including AP and CLEP, community college and online classes, and other opportunities, it is completely possible to graduate from college at the age most teens are graduating from high school. Two of my sons have taken this route—one graduated with a bachelor's degree at twenty, and the other graduated at nineteen. Acceleration doesn't just save time, it can save thousands of dollars in college costs. It's well worth it!

Career Sampling. In traditional school, you're lucky to get one day off each year to shadow a worker at his or her job. Homeschooled teens can try different careers through informal mentoring relationships, formal apprenticeships, or volunteering opportunities. Although formal internships and other programs exist, it is possible to make private arrangements for a teen to volunteer in the workplace. It is easiest to begin with personal friends and acquaintances with potentially interesting careers, but it is possible to approach strangers with a polite business letter and a resume. Career sampling is a wonderful way to try out a job before committing to several years of college or other training. You can think of it as the Goldilocks option!

These are just a few of the many options open to teens who are homeschooled. The thing I have most enjoyed about homeschooling my boys through high school and into college is seeing them develop as individuals. Without excessive scheduling or peer pressure, they were free to learn things they really wanted to know, to sample small business ideas and careers without the pressure of having to immediately earn enough to live on, and to get a jump start on life by accelerating through high school and college. There's nothing more exciting than seeing your teen become the person he or she wants to be!

See more from, and about, Janice in Chapter 10.

☞ *"A World of Options" Resources*

14

Getting Truly Critical

Text and Illustrations by Cathi-Lyn Dyck

Homeschooling is about freedom. It gives you a freer schedule. It gives you a freer, if different, social life. It also gives you the opportunity to cultivate intellectual freedom. "What?!?" you say. "But my kid's four years old! His version of intellectual freedom is dangerous to my mental health!" Yeah, I know. Been there. Four times. But it's not like that forever. If you're reading this book, you want your child to have not just a collection of facts, but, as the popular credo says, "the wisdom to know the difference."

"Did you see how those children behave? And 800 of them, what was she thinking?"

What is critical thinking, precisely? I can tell you it's *not* the two elderly neighbors peering over my back fence and saying, "Would you look at that child? Tsk, tsk. And what is that on her mother's head? Not eggs again??" (Just kidding. I don't have any elderly neighbors.)

Essentially I realized that each subject area is not a collection of related facts and skills which is largely how I taught in the public schools. Each subject area is a method of reasoning to analyze the world around us. We strive to learn the vocabulary of the subject, its history and its purpose. We practice using the subject area to advance our own knowledge. —
Dana Hanley, Principled Discovery[1]

We've all heard about the difference between "knowing what to think" and "knowing how to think." The point is not to just passively receive pre-edited information, but to know how to go out and get what you need. In an article from *www.freeinquiry.com,* Steven D. Schafersman points out the following:

> *It seems obvious that when the information content of a discipline increases, it becomes even more vital to spend time, not learning more information, but learning methods to acquire, understand, and evaluate this information and the great amount of new information that is not known now but will surely follow.*[2]

Critical thinking can be taught formally or by example and discussion, and there are varieties and shades within the discipline. For myself, I was taught unschooled-guerrilla-world-changer critical thinking. It could be summed up in two words: *Question Everything.*

Subject areas are simply arbitrary tools for advancing our own knowledge. They aren't an end in themselves. In fact, "subjects" are subject to a greater framework. Let's look at four components of current North American thinking.

Assumptions

Though I'm not a fan of *The Simpsons,* one of my all-time favorite T-shirts featured Homer with the caption, "Facts are meaningless. They can be used to prove anything." Not too surprisingly, it was gracing the chest of a media employee.

Assumptions are the things we assume to be true in order to help us sort out the value or comparable "truth" of information we encounter. Facts themselves don't help us know what to think. "There was a traffic accident at 32nd Street and Riverdale" is a fact. What you think or feel about it is something else. We use prior assumptions to give meaning to facts. They form a default filtering system for sorting information. But how clogged is your filter?

The question "why" is the most important one out there, not just in your young child's vocabulary, but in your own. As adults, particularly after spending a number of years in institutional settings such as school and workplace, we lose the why reflex. Do you stop to question what people intend to convey, or do you simply take the words as you understand them? Do you think about why you make those conclusions?

Well, none of us usually do. However, that's the fastest way to start training yourself in basic critical thinking skills. The website *Mission: Critical*[3] puts it this way: "The job of a critical thinker is to understand the statements *as they were meant,* rather than insisting on a purely literal construction."

1) When a cigarette manufacturer runs an ad campaign focused on educating kids about the dangers of smoking, do you say, "Well, at least that's something," and dismiss it, or do you talk about it with your kids? Do you look at the assumptions of the marketplace, or are they fairly irrelevant to daily conversation? You can examine the assumptions of public relations campaigns and learn to effectively challenge them by refusing to conform to the results they're attempting to get from people.

2) You can look at thrift shops for old textbooks or encyclopaedias and compare their information to what's taught this year. What are the assumptions people used back then or are using today? Do you know what the assumptions of our culture used to be, or are you assuming the information you have about that time period is accurate and complete? Have you taken into account the assumptions of those who provided the information you rely upon?

I know. Isn't it freaky? Assumptions relate not just to how we think about information, but *information about information.* Is there a way to cut through the chaos?

Yes. ☆ ***The key is to remember that critical thinking doesn't just study what's been said, it looks deeper to what's meant.*** Language is supposed to be a system of sounds with agreed-upon meanings, but in real life, it's not. In studying religion or politics, you learn that groups tend to modify the meaning of words. This runs deeper than assumptions. It goes back to what creates them.

Before the American Civil War, it was assumed by a large part of the culture that it was okay to enslave Africans and drag them halfway around the world to work for no pay against their will. Now, by the way I phrased that sentence, you can tell what my contrasting assumption is. But what's the basis for my assumption? What did the slave-traders base their assumptions on? How did they reason in favor of their behavior? There's more to an assumption than just assuming things are so.

Basis

What's a basis? It's a solid reason for holding a position. But what makes a good basis? What's the difference between a fact and an opinion?

A fact is something that can be confirmed or denied by the direct observation of other people. But then, what about the facts of history? All we can do is evaluate the observations of those who were there, when they haven't been destroyed by time, in the best way we know how. Dana Hanley says, "When I teach, we use authentic literature ('living books'), and primary source materials whenever possible. We copy experts in the field to learn to study math, history, science, art, etc."[4]

Does every witness see the same factual events? The court system will tell you no. Different people observe different things about the same event. This brings us back to evaluating not just what's said, but what's meant by it. It's an easy principle to remember.

A worldview is just that—it's how you view the world. Another word is bias, though that doesn't cover all the aspects of it. Worldview isn't just what you feel is true, but what qualities you believe truth has. Everyone has a sense of truth, but it's not often we stop to think about where it came from.

Critical thinking helps you refine your worldview into a tool of personal power. It doesn't tell you what to do with that understanding. You'll use supporting reasons to help you figure out the basis for your actions. Are your supporting reasons based on facts, emotions, experience or what you've been taught? Have you subjected the facts

"I hate his politics! Do an exposé on him! Make up facts if you have to!! No one reads journalistic correction notices anyway . . . ."

as you understand them to critical examination? Are the values and beliefs that motivate you in conflict with observable, confirmed facts?

Teaching this sort of self-examination helps kids to move beyond what they feel at the moment (though not at the age of four!), and make clearheaded decisions about the information and the choices presented to them.

Values and Beliefs

Having learned how to pick out an assumption, how do you figure out where the assumption itself came from?

Everyone has a set of values that controls their basic assumptions about daily life. Values are shaped by parents, peers, relatives, experiences, personal beliefs and culture. Even your personal philosophy about how you want your kids to form values is guided by . . . yep. Assumptions driven by underlying values.

We use the terms "values" and "beliefs" interchangeably at times, but in fact they're separate things. Beliefs refer to what we hold to be true guiding principles, while values refer to the moral weight we give to things. Moral values are defined by a person's belief system.

The deconstruction of values (other people's, that is) is a popular hobby amongst many groups. Every part of society has its criticisms about the rest of the country. It's challenging and even enjoyable to learn and compare the underlying assumptions and values that lead different groups to their often-loudly-stated conclusions.

Again, some examples.

1) Gay marriage was recently made lawful in Canada. It's the subject of ongoing debate in the States. Each side of the debate holds several assumptions about a variety of areas: morality, religious freedoms, human rights and unlawful discrimination. What values are behind those assumptions? How do you know? What values allow for the assumption that each side can or should use abrasive terminology (as often happens) to portray the other side's goals and values? What values form the assumption that various groups can or should try to regulate or influence other people's actions or their beliefs?

2) Everyone knows someone who holds a spiritual belief of some sort. You may know others who have changed belief systems. What shift of values do they talk about experiencing? What shift of values and assumptions do you observe in their lives? What influences do they mention? What values and beliefs of your own shape your assumptions about the information they communicate?

Desires

Over the last century, North America has moved away from a culture where certain ideas were assumed to be objective, factual and truthful. It has shifted to one where values-oriented "truths" have become subjective and self-determined.

In our culture, choosing beliefs is about what you *want* to choose. Arguments can be found to debunk any belief system, though very rarely are they reasoned out using principles of logic. Because our culture lacks a standardized system of reasoning, wisdom asks that we question motivations. Not just what they are, but how they are created.

We need to be able to recognize the difference between thinking that feeds its own assumptions and thinking that honestly questions them. You use your desires, beliefs, values and the assumptions they require to shape your view of the facts. You need to know the toolkit is in working order.

Believing something simply because it sounds good to us makes us gullible. As advertisers know, all that remains is for someone to *convince us of what we want.* Then, with a little helpful editing of our values, it's time to head down the garden path to the *Brand New Assumptions Store.* This will be followed closely by a trip to *My Little Shoppe of Pre-Fabricated Conclusions.* It's very easy to do an end run around our "intellectually free" society when it becomes free of intellect.

This doesn't matter at all if your philosophy of life doesn't affect anything about how you live. But if that's the case, why do you have a philosophy? And is it your true system of thought, or just a smokescreen to keep your actual beliefs from facing questioning? Those are questions you want your kids to learn to ask for their own safety, happiness and success. Let's personalize.

1) Your ten-year-old's best friend drops by after supper. The boys get into an intense conversation out on the front step, and your son finds out that his friend has joined a gang. How does your son evaluate this choice and the pressure to make the same choice? How does he reflect on his desires and their influence on his choices?

2) Your thirteen-year-old daughter is feeling pressured by her fifteen-year-old boyfriend to have sex. How does she evaluate his attempts at persuasion? How does she evaluate her own desires?

3) Your sixteen-year-old is driving some friends around after school. Somebody pulls out a flask and a baggie of pills. How does your kid determine how to deal with this? How does he think about what he wants at the moment and what effect it has on his judgment?

The endgame: ★ ***Find the most beneficial, useful and empowering place and function of the four components of worldview.***

But how do you even get started?

Starting Young

The getting of information has to be doable before you can begin sorting out all these complex elements. Let's pause for a moment to remember the three thought tools Schafersman mentioned:

1) Acquiring

2) Understanding

3) Evaluating

Based on the examples I gave above, I feel it's best to start them thinking about the world at a young age. It's not hard. You just don't start with the abstract stuff.

At a very early age, you can start talking about what people see, hear, taste, touch and smell. Those are things that other people can experience too. Other people can't see or taste your feelings and thoughts. You can talk about object-words (that describe things) and feeling-words (that ask you to feel something about the things described).

Use source materials. You can demonstrate the type of critical thinking needed for gathering information by giving your kids the resources to find out more about things they're interested in and showing them how to use those resources. Reading to them every day seems like a small thing, but they get it ingrained that books open new worlds of thought. By example, you're teaching them that they can get information for themselves. Helping them use a dictionary, a thesaurus, or telling them, "Look it up!" encourages information-gathering. It also lightens the homeschooling load when they start teaching themselves! The skills to look things up need to be shown by example until your kids have a good grasp of how to do it themselves.

My six-year-old daughter trusts that everything I tell her about life is true and accurate, but I don't want her to be stuck at that level forever. Rather than just relying on "spoon-fed" information, I want her to be able to decipher who to trust for information as she grows older. That means making it possible for her to find her own information and check up on people. It also means teaching understanding.

My husband can look at a type of engine he's never seen before, and within a few minutes, he'll say, "Oh, I understand!" That's because he's acquired enough information about the principles of combustion engines—what parts they require in order to work, for instance —that he can apply that information to varying setups. I can't do that, because I don't have the necessary information to help me understand why an engine is the way it is.

Study word meanings. You can demonstrate how to understand information beginning with the simple act of saying, "That word means..." It teaches kids that meaning can be gleaned from things they don't understand. It also teaches them that meaning is accessible. Using what they know about information gathering, they can broaden their own understanding. They don't have to get stuck hoping that those who'd like to tell them what to think are really acting in good faith.

Step back and recognize your child's ability to think independently. The best way to teach understanding is not to force yourself to be the person who knows it all. If your kids hear you say, "I don't understand what this means," and then get to watch you figure it out, they'll see how to do it for themselves. If you can't figure out how to figure it out, talk to someone who can tell you. As long as you remain open to their questions, your kids will follow your example of gathering information in order to get on the path to understanding things.

The words, "Does that make sense?" open things up for evaluation. Following that with the question, "Why?" leads the child through the process. Making gentle objections to their reasoning by pointing out facts they already know helps them learn to self-correct their evaluation process. As they grow older, you can begin teaching them debate by throwing in facts they didn't already know, as long as it's not done in a way that makes them feel stupid. Coaching them in sensible, thoughtful responses to new information enriches their ability to understand and evaluate.

Model an investigative, not a judgmental attitude. Listen to how you evaluate events and people. Pay attention to what you think about things. Question your own presuppositions, your assumptions and values. Children get their values primarily from what their parents model. If you model an investigative attitude toward beliefs and values, your kids will follow.

Encourage your kids to dig deeper. One of my favorite questions, and one my kids fire back at me regularly, is, "How do you know?" Another good one is, "Were you there? If not, who was?" These kinds of questions teach them to think about basis in a very concrete way. If the answer is, "Because the book I'm reading says so," you can ask how the writer knows. If the answer is, "But I saw it on TV," you can talk about why it was put on TV.

"Examine all things. Hold fast to that which is good.' Paul of Tarsus, 60 AD . . . Hmm."

Expose them to contrasting viewpoints. As they get older, expose them to two or three contrasting viewpoints on various topics. Look at bias. Think about what makes people like or dislike various things. Talk about evidence and basis for beliefs and attitudes.

The question, "How do you know?" is especially powerful when it comes to beliefs and values. It lifts the discussion out of the muddy waters of personal preference and asks for more from life. With the tools to gather more information, to understand it and to evaluate it, the societal forces that pressure your kids can be checked for broken parts and handed back to the people they came from. See if *they* can put it back together.

Cathi-Lyn Dyck is a former unschooled student, visual artist, musician and writer. She lives in Manitoba, Canada with her husband and four children. The Dycks have a twenty-five-acre spread where they produce vegetables, natural honey, wild (but not uncultivated) children, original artwork and music and random helpful writings. You can visit their farm at:

www.mts.net/~lzycre

Jessica's Favorites

Jessica Curry Jobes is now twenty-four. She provided this list for the first edition when she was seventeen. Also see Authors & Poets on page 129.

- Louisa May Alcott: *Little Women* (Civil War period)
- James Boyd: *Drums* (American Revolution)
- Esther Forbes: *Johnny Tremain* (American Revolution)
- Charles Dickens: *The Tale of Two Cities* (French Revolution)
- Alexandre Dumas: *Count of Monte Christo, Edmund Dantes*
- G.A. Henty: *In the Reign of Terror* (French Revolution)
- Victor Hugo: *Les Miserables, The Hunchback of Notre Dame*
- Baroness Orczy: *The Scarlett Pimpernal* (French Revolution)
- Jane Porter: *Thaddeus of Warsaw* (Polish Revolution)
- Henryk Seinkiewicz: *Quo Vadis* (1st Century)
- Sir Walter Scott: *Ivanhoe* (Middle Ages)
- Shakespeare: *The Merchant of Venice* (Renaissance)
- Elizabeth G. Speare: *The Witch of Blackbird Pond* (American Revolutionary period)
- Lew Wallace: *Ben Hur* (1st Century)

Course of Study

One does not have to study any particular topics in any particular grades. When in doubt, do things sequentially: "What happened first in history?" "What was discovered first?" "What in science was first?" "What was written first?" You may use the following for your scope and sequence—especially for the lower grades—or design your own plan. Add topics such as Music and Art, if you like. The grade-level music suggestions herein are from Cathi-Lyn Dyck. For all grades study the lives and music of the suggested composers. Choose high quality "adult" recordings.

This course of study does not necessarily fulfill any college or graduation requirements. For many more topics to choose from, see World Book's *Typical Course of Study* in the parents' section of their site: *www.worldbook.com*.

1st Grade

Social Studies
❑ Local and family history
❑ Simple geographical terms
❑ Making and reading a simple neighborhood map

Science
❑ Nature study
❑ Animals, including birds and habitats
❑ Seeds, bulbs, plants, flowers
❑ Grouping and classification

Language Arts
- ❏ Phonics
- ❏ Enunciation and pronunciation
- ❏ Reading practice (only after mastery of phonics)
- ❏ Creating stories and poems—parent writes down
- ❏ Narration after parent reads
- ❏ Basic punctuation and capitalization
- ❏ Beginning handwriting

Health and Safety
- ❏ Establish habits: hygiene, including dental
- ❏ Caring for home environment—folding laundry, etc.
- ❏ Exercise and rest
- ❏ Nutrition
- ❏ General safety rules

Mathematics
- ❏ Counting and writing to 100
- ❏ Beginning addition and subtraction facts to 5 or 10
- ❏ Concepts of equality and inequality
- ❏ Using 1/2 and 1/4 appropriately

Music
- ❏ Johann Sebastian Bach (1685-1750) and Antonio Vivaldi (1678-1741).

2nd Grade

Social Studies
- ❏ Holidays
- ❏ Acquiring food and food sources
- ❏ World history overview
- ❏ Basic geography: oceans, continents
- ❏ Map use

Science

- ❏ Nature Study
- ❏ Earth and sky
- ❏ Sun, moon, planets
- ❏ Simple constellations
- ❏ Exploring space

Language Arts

- ❏ Reading silently and aloud
- ❏ Alphabetizing, dictionary guide words
- ❏ Handwriting
- ❏ Copywork
- ❏ Narration

Health and Safety

- ❏ Maintain or establish habits: hygiene, dental
- ❏ Basic food groups

Mathematics

- ❏ Counting, reading, writing to 1,000
- ❏ Counting by 2's, 5's, and 10's
- ❏ Addition and subtraction facts to 20
- ❏ Basic multiplication and division facts
- ❏ Weight, length, volume, shape, temperature, time, calendar, charts, graphs

Music

- ❏ Ludwig Van Beethoven (1770-1827) and Wolfgang Amadeus Mozart (1756-1791).

3rd Grade

Social Studies

- ❏ Biographies
- ❏ Local and national geography and topography
- ❏ Flat maps

Science
- ❏ Nature study
- ❏ Plants and animals of the desert
- ❏ Plants and animals of the sea
- ❏ Common birds, trees, flowers
- ❏ Forest plants
- ❏ Conservation

Language Arts
- ❏ Reading silently and aloud
- ❏ Dictation, narration, copywork
- ❏ Dictionary skills
- ❏ Beginning cursive writing
- ❏ Writing short, original stories and poems; editing, proofreading

Health and Safety
- ❏ Maintain or establish habits: hygiene, dental
- ❏ Care of eyes and ears
- ❏ Proper balance of activities
- ❏ The body
- ❏ Nutrition

Mathematics
- ❏ Reading and writing numbers to 99,999
- ❏ Beginning Roman numerals
- ❏ Rounding numbers
- ❏ Addition and subtraction facts to 25
- ❏ Multiplication and division facts to 100
- ❏ Mastery of math facts: flash cards or other drill

Music
- ❏ Fryderyk Chopin (1810-1849), Felix Mendelssohn (1809-1847), Johannes Brahms (1833-1897) and Pyotr Il'ych Tchaikovsky (1840-1893).

4th Grade

Social Studies
- ❏ State history, local customs and music
- ❏ Continents and climatic regions
- ❏ Time zones
- ❏ Using a globe

Science
- ❏ Nature study
- ❏ Insects, mammals, plants, reptiles
- ❏ Environment of the local region
- ❏ Earth and its history
- ❏ Oceans and the hydrosphere
- ❏ Air and water pollution

Language Arts
- ❏ Telephone manners and skills
- ❏ Making and accepting simple social introductions
- ❏ Summarizing simple information
- ❏ Cursive handwriting
- ❏ Simple outlining
- ❏ Developing skills in locating information
- ❏ Writing a report
- ❏ Narration, dictation, copywork

Health and Safety
- ❏ Maintain habits: hygiene, dental
- ❏ Skeletal and muscular systems
- ❏ Care and proper use of the body
- ❏ Principles of digestion
- ❏ Substance abuse

Mathematics
- ❏ *Saxon* Math 54

Music
- ❏ Claude Debussy (1862-1918), Gustav Holst (1874-1934), Sergei Rachmaninov (1873-1943) and Maurice Ravel(1875-1937).

5th Grade

Social Studies
- ❏ Exploration and discovery
- ❏ Settlement
- ❏ Revolutionary period
- ❏ Democracy's principles and documents
- ❏ 1812 War
- ❏ U.S. geography, national resources

Science
- ❏ Animal and plant classification
- ❏ Bacteria
- ❏ Human body

Language Arts
- ❏ Silent and oral reading
- ❏ Homonyms, homophones and homographs, synonyms and antonyms
- ❏ Using a thesaurus
- ❏ Spelling
- ❏ Plurals and possessives
- ❏ Cursive handwriting
- ❏ Preparing a simple bibliography
- ❏ Writing and editing own compositions
- ❏ Using study materials: keys, tables, graphs, charts, legends, library catalogs, index, table of contents, reference materials, maps

Health and Safety
- ❏ Dental hygiene
- ❏ Public works: water, sewage

- ❑ Care of the eyes
- ❑ Nutrition and diet
- ❑ Elementary first aid

Mathematics
- ❑ *Saxon* Math 65

Music
- ❑ Bela Bartok (1881-1945), Scott Joplin (1868-1917), Louis Armstrong (1901-1971) and Oscar Peterson (1925-

6th Grade

Social Studies
- ❑ Pioncers, Westward Movement
- ❑ Industrial, cultural and geographic growth
- ❑ Transportation and communication
- ❑ North and South America
- ❑ Citizenship and social responsibility
- ❑ War between the States
- ❑ Map and globe skills

Science
- ❑ Electricity and magnetism, electronics
- ❑ Sound, light and heat
- ❑ Energy: solar, nuclear, etc.
- ❑ Properties of water
- ❑ Light and color
- ❑ Simple and complex machines

Language Arts
- ❑ Types of literature
- ❑ Using roots, prefixes and suffixes
- ❑ Sentence structure, diagraming
- ❑ Cursive handwriting
- ❑ Writing and editing own compositions

- ❏ Types of writing: narration, description, exposition, persuasion
- ❏ Simple note taking
- ❏ Using reference books and indexes
- ❏ Using electronic reference materials
- ❏ Discerning author's point of view

Health and Safety
- ❏ Personal appearance, hygiene
- ❏ Exercise and fitness
- ❏ The health professions
- ❏ Systems of the human body
- ❏ Human reproduction

Mathematics
- ❏ Saxon 76

Music
- ❏ Learn the sections of the classical orchestra and what instruments are in them. Listen to how different composers used them, from Bach onwards.

7th Grade

Social Studies
- ❏ World History
- ❏ World trade and resources
- ❏ World geography
- ❏ Advanced map and globe skills

Science
- ❏ Composition of the earth
- ❏ Rocks, soil and minerals
- ❏ The earth's movement
- ❏ Conservation
- ❏ Ecosystems, ecology, environment
- ❏ Climate and weather

Language Arts

- ❑ Literature
- ❑ Planning and producing dramatizations
- ❑ Clauses and phrases
- ❑ Compound sentences
- ❑ Writing and editing descriptions, reports, journals, and letters
- ❑ Note taking and outlining
- ❑ Extending reference skills: atlases, directories, encyclopedias, periodicals, on-line information services, CD-ROMs and other electronic reference material
- ❑ Library organization

Health and Safety

- ❑ Good grooming and posture
- ❑ Dental health
- ❑ Healthy habits and lifestyles
- ❑ Exercise and fitness
- ❑ Circulation and respiration
- ❑ Antibiotics
- ❑ Personal and public safety
- ❑ Accident prevention

Mathematics

- ❑ Saxon Math 87

Music

- ❑ Instruments in a marching band. Study and listen to British and American marching bands.

8th Grade

Social Studies

- ❑ Current events
- ❑ Parties and politics
- ❑ Reconstruction to WW II
- ❑ National geography

Science
- ❏ The universe and Milky Way
- ❏ Astronomy
- ❏ Space and space travel
- ❏ Atmosphere
- ❏ Air pressure

Language Arts
- ❏ World poets and storytellers
- ❏ Spelling mastery
- ❏ Infinitive, participle, gerund, predicate nominative, predicate adjective, direct and indirect object
- ❏ Kinds of sentences and their parts
- ❏ Functions of sentence elements

Health and Safety
- ❏ Grooming
- ❏ The body's utilization of food
- ❏ Types and functions of foods
- ❏ Substance abuse

Mathematics
- ❏ *Saxon* Math Algebra 1/2

Music
- ❏ Use the Internet and library to learn about Chinese music—what it sounds like, who were the great Chinese composers

9th Grade

Social Studies
- ❏ Community, state and national government
- ❏ Political parties and elections
- ❏ Elementary economics
- ❏ Labor and management
- ❏ Modern history, post WW II

❑ Democracy vs. Communism

Science
❑ Scientific nomenclature
❑ Lab techniques and safety
❑ Scientific classification
❑ Scientific method

Language Arts
❑ Parable and allegory
❑ Interpretation of literature
❑ Effective discussion techniques and questioning skills
❑ Preparing a speech
❑ Public speaking and debate
❑ Foreign words used in English
❑ Grammar
❑ Fundamentals of composition

Mathematics
❑ *Saxon* Algebra I
❑ Personal and family math

Music
❑ Use the Internet and library to learn about Middle Eastern music

10th Grade

Social Studies
❑ Prehistoric through Renaissance
❑ Classic literature of the periods studied

Science
❑ Biology, including microscopic life
❑ Photosynthesis
❑ Cells

- ❏ Genetics and heredity
- ❏ Environmental issues

Language Arts
- ❏ Novel, short story and essay
- ❏ Poetry: lyric and the sonnet
- ❏ Distinguishing between fact and opinion
- ❏ Persuasion and argumentation
- ❏ Public speaking and debate
- ❏ Dictionary skills
- ❏ Grammar
- ❏ Techniques of writing
- ❏ Writing short stories, poetry and plays
- ❏ Writing term papers
- ❏ Constructing footnotes

Mathematics
- ❏ Saxon Algebra II

Music
- ❏ Use the Internet and library to learn about African music.

11th Grade

Social Studies
- ❏ American history

Science
- ❏ Chemistry

Language Arts
- ❏ American literature
- ❏ Poetry
- ❏ Critical and evaluative reading
- ❏ Vocabulary development
- ❏ Grammar

- ❏ Editorial, journalistic writing
- ❏ Writing term papers
- ❏ Proofreading symbols
- ❏ Use of Reader's Guide and other reference aids, both print and electronic

Mathematics
- ❏ *Saxon* Advanced Math

Music
- ❏ Create a timeline of world composers and learn how they influenced each other, from Bach to Bartok, Africa to New Orleans. Study folk music of the world and how it is transmitted—through oral tradition, through travel.

12th Grade

Social Studies
- ❏ Government: national, and comparative
- ❏ Current events, politics, law
- ❏ National business and industry
- ❏ International relations
- ❏ Democracy vs. Communism
- ❏ World interdependence, problems and issues
- ❏ English and other world history

Science
- ❏ Physics
- ❏ Electronics
- ❏ Nuclear energy
- ❏ Atomic structure

Language Arts
- ❏ English literature, including Shakespeare
- ❏ Literary, social, and political heritage of England
- ❏ World literature

- ❏ Writing term papers

Mathematics
- ❏ Saxon Calculus
- ❏ Computer literacy
- ❏ Family finances

Music
- ❏ Study the physics of music—the relationship between wavelengths of notes in given chords. Use available items like copper piping cut in lengths to examine the ratios. Use fishing line and wooden pegs to do string length ratios. Study the mathematics of music. Use online resources, the library or talk to professors at your nearest university—by phone or email if necessary.

Sample Scope and Sequence

Most concepts can be covered the EasySchool way, with much reading and writing. This is a sample only. Design your own special scope and sequence!

Grade 3

I. *Social Studies*
   A. World humanitarian projects
   B. World religions overview
   C. Geography
      1. European
      2. African
   D. Review Egypt, Greece, Rome, Middle Ages
   E. Renaissance, Reformation, beyond.

II. *Science*
   A. Meteorology
   B. Men and women of science

III. *Language Arts*
   A. Reading
      1. Classic children's poets
      2. *McGuffey's* readers
   B. Writing
      1. Stories
      2. Poems
   C. Penmanship
   D. Speech

          1. Enunciation

          2. Memory work

   E. Mechanics of language

          1. Spelling

          2. Grammar

          3. Punctuation

IV. *Health*

   A. Organs

   B. Prevention and safety

   C. Men and women of health

V. *Mathematics*

   A. *Practical Arithmetics* text

   B. Facts drill

   C. Story problems

Class Schedule Planner

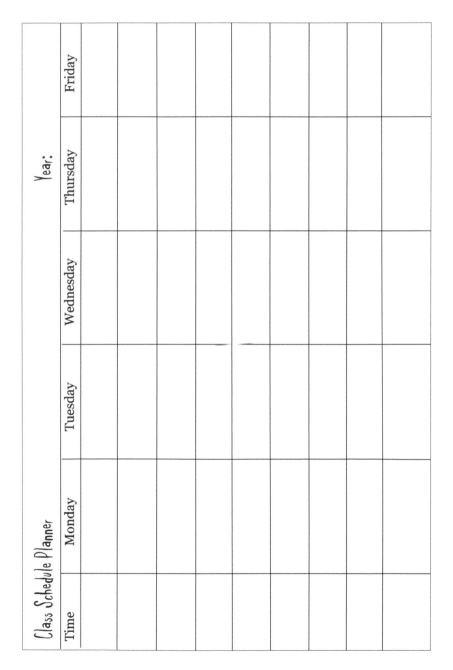

Time	Monday	Tuesday	Wednesday	Thursday	Friday

Class Schedule Planner

Year:

Resources

Preface

Easy Homeschooling
402 Wausa Rd
Boelus NE 68820
308-996-4497
Fax: 308-996-9104
info@easyhomeschooling.com
www.easyhomeschooling.com
FREE Copywork, checklists, articles, newsletter.

F.U.N. Books
PO Box 1360
Pasadena MD 21123-1360
Fax/Voice 410-360-7330
Orders: 888-386-7020
FUN@FUN-Books.com
www.FUN-Books.com

Home Education Magazine
PO Box 1083
Tonasket WA 98855-1083
Orders: 800-236-3278
HEM@homeedmaga.com
www.homeedmag.com

The Successful Homeschool Family Handbook
The Moore Foundation
PO Box 98
North Bonneville WA 98639
509-427-7779
Orders: 800-891-5255
Fax: 509-427-7772
moorehomeschool@yahoo.com
www.moorefoundation.com
Better Late Than Early, School Can Wait and others.

Chapter 2

Home School Legal Defense Association
PO Box 3000
Purcellville VA 20134-9000
540-338-5600
Fax: 540-338-2733
info@hslda.org
www.hslda.org/laws/default.asp

Home School Manual
Gazelle Publications
11560 Red Bud Trail
Berrien Springs MI 49103
800-650-5076
info@gazellepublications.com
www.gazellepublications.com

Dover Publications, Inc.
31 E 2nd St
Mineola NY 11501-3852
Fax: 516-742-6953
www.doverpublications.com

Alpha-Phonics

phonics@howtotutor.com

www.alpha-phonics.com

Simply Phonics

Shoelace Books

shoelacebooks@yahoo.com

Scholastic Inc.

800-724-6527

www.scholastic.com

Chapter 3

Saxon Publishers

www.saxonpublishers.com

Chapter 4

Don Aslett's Cleaning Center

311 South 5th Avenue

Pocatello ID 83201

208-232-6212

Fax: 208-235-5481

www.cleanreport.com

Chapter 5

Course of Study
Scope and Sequence
Class Schedule Planner

All located in this section of the book.

Chapter 6

National Gallary of Art
National Lending Service
2000B South Club Drive
Landover MD 20785
202-842-6822
Fax: 202-789-3246
www.nga.gov/education/education.htm

Kids Art
PO Box 274
Mt Shasta CA 96067
530-926-5076
Fax: 530-926-0851
info@kidsart.com
www.kidsart.com

Dr. Raymond Moore
See The Moore Foundation, "Preface," above.

Simply Phonics
See Chapter 2, "Starting Up" above.

Chapter 7

The Lester Family
PO Box 203
Joshua Tree CA 92252
760-366-1023
info@lesterfamilymusic.com
www.lesterfamilymusic.com

Home School Treasures
454 Covenant Street
Bethlehem GA 30620
678-425-0150
info@hstreasures.com
http://www.hstreasures.com

Exceptional Books
www.easyhomeschooling.com/rare-antique-books.html

Chapter 8

Naomi Aldort's Recommended Reading
- Aldort, Naomi. *Raising Our Children, Raising Ourselves,* Book Publisher's Network, 2006.
- Greenberg, Daniel. *Free at Last,* Sudbury Valley School Press, 1987.
- Holt, John. *Escape from Childhood,* New York: E. P. Dutton, 1974.
- Holt, John. *How Children Learn,* New York: Dell, 1972.
- Holt, John. *Learning All the Time,* Reading, MA: Addison-Wesley, 1989.
- Alfie Kohn, *Punished by Rewards,* Houghton Mifflin Com pany 1993

Chapter 9

Art Teaching Books
- *Drawing Textbook*
- *Drawing with Children*
- *The Beginning of Creativity*
- *Usborne Guide to Drawing*

National Gallery of Art
See above, Chapter 6, "Combining Subjects."

Math Writing Books
By Marilyn Burns
- *Math and Literature*
- *The I Hate Mathematics! Book*

Bookstores, libraries, *www.amazon.com*. Other resources by Marilyn Burns are available from ETA/Cuisenaire, 800-445-5985, www.etacuisenaire.com

Typical Course of Study
www.worldbook.com/wb/Students?curriculum

Chapter 11

Classical Homeschooling
The Well-Trained Mind
Peace Hill Press
18101 The Glebe Lane
Charles City VA 23030
WebAdmin@welltrainedmind.com
www.welltrainedmind.com

The Charlotte Mason Research and Supply Co.
PO Box 296
Quarryville PA 17566
www.charlottemason.com

F.U.N. News
Home Education Magazine
The Successful Homeschool Family Handbook
See "Preface" above.

Home School Treasures
See Chapter 7, above.

Chapter 12

Business Books
From your library, or any bookstore.
- *Homemade Money,* Barbara Brabec
- *Guerrilla Marketing,* Jay Conrad Levinson

F.U.N. Books
See "Preface" above.

HomeGrown Business
www.BiblicalWomanhood.com/homegrown.htm

Once-A-Month Cooking
- *Once-A-Month Cooking* by Mary Beth Lagerborg, Mimi Wilson
- *Frozen Assets* by Deborah Taylor-Hough

Chapter 13

Home School High School & Beyond
Castlemoyle Books
The Hotel Revere Building
694 Main Street
Pomeroy WA 99347
Orders: 888-SPELL-86
509-843-5009
Fax: 509-843-6098
johnr@castlemoyle.com
http://www.castlemoyle.com

Dinner's in the Freezer!
Also *Mega Cooking,* both by Jill Bond
www.amazon.com

A World of Options
- *7 Habits of Highly Effective Teens*, Sean Covey
- *Working From Home*, Paul and Sarah Edwards *www.sba.gov*
- *Europe Through the Back Door*, Rick Steves
- *Get a Jump Start on College!* Janice Campbell
  www.doingcollegeyourway.com
- *Do What You Are,* Paul Tieger and Barbara Barron-Tieger
  www.dowhatyouare.com

Other Resources

Children's Books
PO Box 239
Greer SC 29652
Orders: 800-344-3198
Questions: 864-968-0391
www.childsbooks.com

Homeschooling Horizons Magazine
42 Prevost RR 7
Vaudreuil-Dorion (QC) J7V 8P5
Canada
450-424-3222
staff@homeschoolinghorizons.com
www.homeschoolinghorizons.com

Web Freebies

⇒ *www.easyhomeschooling.com* Over 40 pages of
resources, including copywork, checklists, articles,
ebooks and newsletter issues.

⇒ *www.toytowntreasures.com* Over 40
worksheets.

⇒ *www.redshift.com/~bonajo/vocabbingo.htm*
Vocabulary Bingo Card Generator. You put in your
own list of vocabulary words and definitions and it
generates various bingo cards from your personal list.
You can use it for a multitude of applications—states
& capitals, history dates, artists and their paintings,
mountains or rivers and their locations, etc.

⇒ w*ww.deepspringspress.com* Science lessons,
forms and guides.

⇒*www.paideaclassics.org*
Classic literature e-texts,
homeschool planning pages,
handwriting, copywork,
spelling curriculum and
more.

⇒ ***www.HandsofaChild.com*** Science and history. K-9 grade level.

⇒ ***www.synapses.co.uk/merlin/index.html*** The first part of three science courses.

⇒ ***www.naomialdort.com*** Articles about unschooling, parenting advice columns.

⇒ ***www.shillermath.com*** Math articles.

⇒ ***www.EverydayEducation.com*** Free GPA Calculator, more.

⇒ ***www.ArtofEloquence.com*** Free sample chapter of each of several communication studies as well as some free communication activities.

⇒ ***www.thehomeschoolmom.com*** Free Spanish lessons, homeschool planner and organizer, lesson plans, unit studies, software downloads, information, articles, dinner menus—with recipes and grocery lists, more.

⇒ ***www.edhelper.com*** Worksheets on many different subjects and topics.

⇒ ***www.bellaonline.com/articles/art35103.asp*** Creative writing prompts

⇒ ***www.bellaonline.com/articles/art12709.asp*** Science ideas and links.

⇒ ***www.authorama.com*** Public domain electronic books.

⇒ *www.amblesideonline.org* Charlotte Mason curriculum guide and booklists.

⇒ *www.homeschoolmath.net* Worksheet generator.

⇒ *www.homeschoolnewslink.com* Free national homeschool newspaper, *The Link*.

⇒ *www.schoolexpress.com* Wide assortment of freebies.

→ *www.unitstudyhelps.com/freebies.shtml* Several links to various freebies.

⇒ *www.chartjungle.com* Printable charts for chores and more.

⇒ *www.simplycharlottemason.com* Articles on narrating and copywork. Free scope and sequence.

Endnotes

Preface

1 Bill Greer, "What is 'Unschooling'?" *F.U.N. News,* October 1994, p. 1.

2 Helen Hegener, editorial, *Home Education Magazine.*

3 Raymond and Dorothy Moore, *The Successful Homeschool Family Handbook: A Creative and Stress-Free Approach to Homeschooling* (Thomas Nelson, 1994).

4 [71.1%] Dr. Brian Ray, and the Home School Legal Defense Association, 1997.

Chapter 1
Laying Foundations

1 The method for setting and reaching goals described in this book was adapted from that of businessman Charles Givens.

2 Charlotte Mason, *An Essay towards a Philosophy of Education* (Wheaton: Tyndale House 1989).

3 William Feather, *Living Quotations for Christians* (New York: Harper & Row, 1974) p. 63.

Chapter 2
Starting Up

1 It is important that young children are not pushed into formal schooling too soon. See any of Dr. Raymond and Dorothy Moore's books, especially *Better Late than Early* or *School Can Wait.*

2   Lyric Wallwork Winik, "We are Responsible," *Parade Magazine,* March 19, 1995, p. 7.

3   *The Futurist,* January-February 1996 (World Future Society, 7910 Woodmont Ave., Suite 450, Bethesda, MD 20814, 301-656-8274, fax: 301-951-0394).

4   "Science Fiction," Zane CD Rom.

5   William F. Russell, *Classics to Read Aloud to Your Children,* 1984.

6   Lyric Wallwork Winik, "We are Responsible," *Parade Magazine,* March 19, 1995, p. 7.

Chapter 3
Easy School Basics

1   *Strong Families, Strong Schools,* DOE, 1995.

Chapter 4
Making Order

1   Personal correspondence.

Chapter 7
Enjoying Heirlooms

1   Sherman County Times (Loup City NE, 1924).

2   Arthur Robinson Ph.D., The Robinson Self-Teaching Home School Curriculum (Oregon Institute of Science and Medicine and Althouse Press, 1997).

3   James Kilpatrick, *The Idaho Statesman*, December 21, 1989, p. 8A.

Chapter 8
The Price of Praise

1   John Holt, *How Children Fail* (New York: Pitman Publishing, 1964), p. xiii.

2   Alice Miller, *The Drama of the Gifted Child* (New York: Basic Books, 1983), p. 104.

3   This story appears in the book, *Raising Our Children, Raising Ourselves* by Naomi Aldort

Chapter 9
Studying Science, Math, and Art

1   Claude Monet, *Modern Masters,* National Gallery of Art.

2   Ron Ranson, *Fast and Loose* video.

3   Marilyn Burns, "The 12 Most Important Things You Can Do to Be a Better Math Teacher," "Math Questions, Ask Marilyn Burns!" "Writing in Math Class, Absolutely!" *Instructor,* April 1993, April 1994, April 1995.

Chapter 10
Teaching Writing

1   Charlotte Mason, *Home Education.* (Wheaton, Illinois: Tyndale House, 1989) p. 227.

2   Ibid.

3   Ibid., p. 241.

4   Ibid.

5   Ibid., p. 242.

6   Ibid., p. 241.

7   Benjamin Franklin, *The Autobiography, Part One. The Norton Anthology of American Literature: Volume A.* Ed. Nina Baym. (New York: W.W. Norton & Company, 2003) p. 547-548.

Chapter 11
Mining Methods and History

1   Douglas Wilson, Wes Callihan, and Douglas Jones, *Classical Education & the Home School,* (Moscow: Canon Press).

2   Wilson, Callihan, and Jones.

3   Wes Callihan, "A Map for the Mind," *Practical Homeschooling,* Issue #24.

4   Ibid.

5   Charlotte Mason, *An Essay towards a Philosophy of Education,* (Wheaton: Tyndale House 1989).

6   Mary Hood, Ph.D., personal correspondence, July 4, 1999.

7   Hood, F.U.N. News, 1995.

8 Dr. Raymond and Dorothy Moore, *The Successful Homeschool Family Handbook,* Thomas Nelson, 1994.
9 Ibid.

Chapter 13
Sailing through High School
1 Mary Hood, Ph.D., *The Relaxed Home School,* p 87.
2 Charlotte Mason, *An Essay towards a Philosophy of Education,* (Wheaton: Tyndale House 1989).

Chapter 14
Getting Truly Critical

1 Dana Hanley, "My Educational Philosophy," June 29, 2006, *http://gottsegnet.blogspot.com/2006/06/my-educational-philosophy-part-iii.html*
2 Stephen D. Schafersman, "An Introduction to Critical Thinking" 1991. *http://www.freeinquiry.com/critical-thinking.html*
3 Mission: Critical can be found at *http://www2.sjsu.edu/depts/itl/index.html.* Site includes detailed explanations and interactive tutorials in critical thinking.
4 Dana Hanley, "My Educational Philosophy," June 29, 2006, *http://gottsegnet.blogspot.com/2006/06/my-educational-philosophy-part-iii.html*

Index

U

V

W

Y

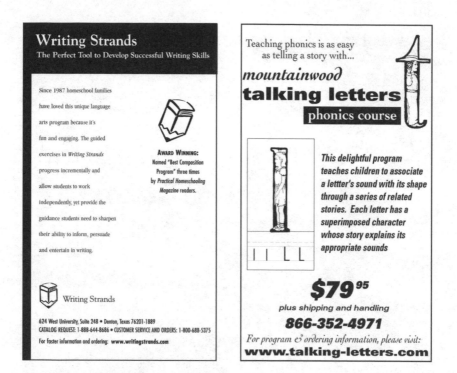

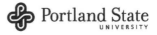

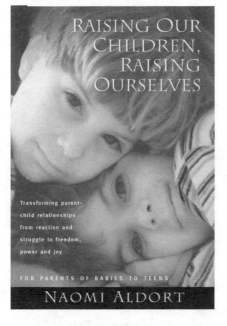

Why Latin?

* ❖ Learn the wisdom of the ancients
* ❖ Learn the Greco-Roman basis of today's Western cultures
* ❖ Learn the foundation for other foreign languages
* ❖ Improve English vocabulary
* ❖ Improve study skills and test scores
* ❖ Learn ancient history and culture

Studies conducted by the *Educational Testing Service* show that Latin students consistently outperform all other students on the verbal portion of the *Scholastic Assessment Test* (SAT).

	2001	2002	2003	2004	2005	2006
Latin	665	666	672	674	681	672
All Students	506	504	507	508	508	503
French	633	637	638	642	643	637
German	625	622	626	627	637	632
Spanish	583	581	575	575	573	577
Hebrew	628	629	628	630	620	623

2006 Taken from Table 21 in College-Bound Seniors — Group Profile Report.

Why the *Artes Latinae* Latin course?

Artes Latinae is...

* ❖ Self-teaching
* ❖ Comprehensive
* ❖ Interactive
* ❖ Self-pacing
* ❖ Flexible
* ❖ Connected
* ❖ Successful

Winner of several **Reader's Choice Awards**
from *Practical Homeschooling Magazine*

"Artes Latinae *has a proven track record of helping students from middle school through graduate school learn Latin on their own . . . .*"
Prof. John Gruber-Miller
CALICO Journal

www.**ArtesLatinae**.com
E-mail: mbolchazy@bolchazy.com

Homeschooling at the Speed of Life

Marilyn Rockett's latest book, Homeschooling at the Speed of Life (B&H Publishing Group, 2007), will be out April 1, 2007 and is available now for pre-publication purchase on www.Amazon.com.

Visit Marilyn's website at www.MarilynRockett.com or contact her at Marilyn@MarilynRockett.com.

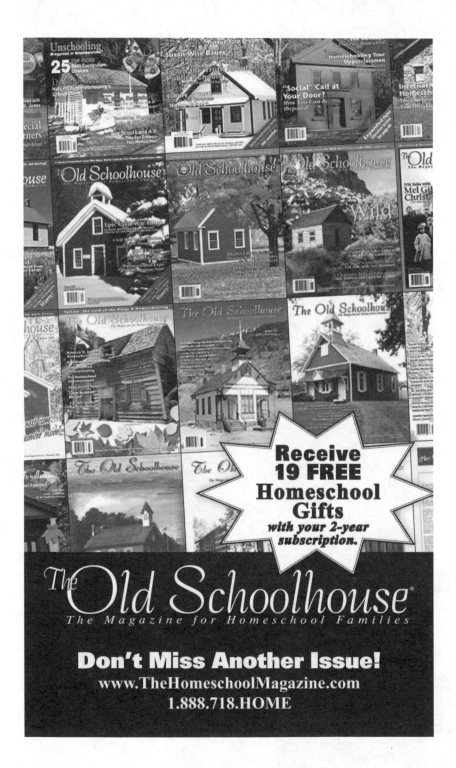